A DEADLY CASE OF
MISTAKEN IDENTITY

The Texans were on the prod and eager for a hanging.

"Just hold up a minute," Longarm told the trail boss. "I think I have something here that will prove you've got the wrong man."

As Longarm spoke, he reached cautiously into his inside coat pocket for his wallet and the badge he kept in it.

"Hey! Watch out!" a rider called. "He's goin' for another belly gun!"

The one with the rope dropped the loop over Longarm's head, turned his horse and lifted it to a gallop. . . .

*Also in the LONGARM series
from Jove*

TABOR EVANS

LONGARM

AND THE PAWNEE KID

JOVE BOOKS, NEW YORK

LONGARM AND THE PAWNEE KID

A Jove Book / published by arrangement with
the author

PRINTING HISTORY
Jove edition / February 1990

ISBN: 0-515-10241-5

Chapter 1

From the ridge Longarm saw the prairie stretching eastward before him, a seemingly endless expanse of grass extending clear to Omaha. Pawnee country. No trimmings shortgrass prairie, flat as a drum head. Due east lay the trail town of Pawnee Wells, an island in a sea of grass. Two days earlier he'd gotten off the Union Pacific train in Grand Island, where he'd picked up the livery mount he was riding. It was now coming on to the close of a weary day in the saddle and he looked forward to making camp in the foothills below, close by the stream he saw winking at him through the tops of the cottonwoods lining both banks. He urged his mount forward and angled down the long slope, leaning back in his saddle to ease the horse's load.

Ducking his head, he rode through the cottonwoods to the stream's bank, dismounted, and unsaddled and

1

hobbled the horse, then peeled off his clothes and dove into the stream. He splashed around in the icy shallows for a while, rubbing off the trail dust and grime with a yellow bar of soap. After ducking under the surface a couple of times to rinse himself off, he reached out to pull himself back up onto the bank when a young man in a sheepskin jacket stepped out from behind one of the trees crowding the bank, an amused smile on his face— and Longarm's .44 in his hand.

"Ain't no need for you to hurry out of that bath, mister," he said.

"As you can see, I'm not armed," Longarm replied. "Put down the gun."

"Just a precaution. I'm a peaceable man by nature and don't want no trouble."

The stranger hunkered down so that he was at Longarm's eye level. His straight shoulder-length black hair, high cheekbones, sharp blade of a nose and swarthy complexion left no doubt of his Indian heritage. Only his blue eyes, glowing spookily in the shadow of his Stetson's straight brim, betrayed his white blood.

"Speaking plainly, mister," the breed said, "I need a hoss and you got one."

"We can share the horse. You'll get less trouble from me if you do."

"Point is, I want to save *you* trouble."

Longarm made no effort to understand that crack as the half-breed stepped back, waggling Longarm's .44 at him as he did so. "Come on out of that water now and put something on. You'll catch your death."

As Longarm stepped up onto the bank he saw his horse, already saddled, waiting behind the half-breed,

2

his own bedroll tied securely behind the cantle.

"Jesus, stranger. You taking everything?"

"Nope. I ain't takin' your clothes." He grinned. "They won't fit."

Longarm stood up, towering over the breed, water streaming off his powerful frame, his eyes smoky with anger. "Now, look," he said, as reasonably as he could manage, "you can't leave a man out here without a horse."

"Just keep on going, follow this stream. You'll hit Sand Creek late tomorrow."

Fuming, Longarm pulled on his long johns. "That don't happen to be where I'm heading."

"I'm real sorry about that. And I wish I didn't have to take your hoss. But I just ain't got no choice."

Longarm glanced at him, surprised. The funny thing was the breed actually did sound sorry. Longarm went back to pulling on his pants. It was not easy with him sopping wet. He buttoned his fly, then put on his shirt and reached down for his vest. He took hold of the watch chain folded neatly on top of it, and in a single deft flick of his wrist, flipped the derringer out of the vest pocket up into his palm. The breed was too quick for him, however, and stepping close, clubbed Longarm on the back of his head with the .44. Longarm went down hard, the derringer falling from his hands.

The breed turned and vaulted, Indian fashion, onto Longarm's horse.

Longarm was down but not out. He shook his head to clear out the cobwebs and as the breed turned the horse and dug his spurs into its flanks, Longarm snatched up the derringer. Still prone, he tracked the breed and fired.

3

The breed twisted in the saddle as if something had pushed him in the side, managed to stay on the horse and vanished into the cottonwoods.

Cursing bitterly, Longarm got to his feet and finished dressing. Strapping his empty cross-draw rig on, he plunged his hat down upon his throbbing skull and set out through the gathering dusk. He was too angry to make camp now, and besides he had nothing to make camp with; and if he were to travel on foot to Sand Creek, he'd sure as hell go a lot farther under the moon's light than that of the boiling sun.

He had not gone far when he heard a storm of hooves coming from the other side of the stream. Longarm halted. He heard horses plunging into the shallow water, their shoes sucking mud as they gained the near side and thundered up onto the bank just ahead of him. As Longarm stood there, a hard-driving band of ten or more riders—Texas drovers from the look of them—broke from the cottonwoods and bore down on him.

"There he is, Mac," one of them cried. "Over there! Look!"

"Yep, that's the one," another said, drawing his iron as he galloped closer.

Cautiously, not wanting to rile anyone, Longarm raised his hands slightly as the riders rode up to him.

"You've rustled your last herd, mister," said one of the Texans, reining up in front of Longarm. He had pure white hair showing under his hat brim and a face almost raw from the sun and wind. His eyes were cold blue slits as he regarded Longarm. He was the oldest of the bunch and obviously the trail boss.

"You men are making a mistake," Longarm told him.

4

"You got me mixed up with someone else."

"You're the one made the mistake, mister, rustling my trail herd."

Another rider pulled his horse to a halt alongside the trail boss. His hands resting on his saddle horn, he asked Longarm, "You got a side arm?"

"Nope."

"How come?"

"Someone took it."

He glanced at the trail boss and smiled, then looked back down at Longarm. "Is that your story?"

"It's no story. It happens to be the truth."

Another rider came to a halt close by Longarm. A coiled loop of rope dangled from his right hand.

"Who took it, mister?" this one asked. "The Man in the Moon?"

"A half-breed. Just now."

The trail boss spoke up then, calmly, soberly, as if he were a judge delivering a sentence. "When we came on your camp this morning, mister, you lit out so quick you left your iron, your rifle, and the rest of your gear behind. We been tracking you all day, and a little while back we found the horse you rode into the ground on the other side of the stream back there. You're the son of a bitch we're after, all right."

"Listen now," Longarm told them. "And listen good. I never rustled any of your cattle. And I never saw a single one of you men before. You've mistaken me for someone else."

"Have we now?" said the trail boss.

"Yes, you have."

"Why're you out here afoot then?"

"Because the man you're after stole my horse."

"I see. He took your gun and stole your horse."

"You expect us to believe such a cock-and-bull story?" the rider with the rope asked.

"You heard my shot, didn't you?"

"No, we didn't hear no shot."

"Well, if you had, that was me shooting at the bastard who took my horse. I think I might've winged him."

Another rider shucked his hat back off his forehead and spat a gob of tobacco juice at Longarm's feet. "Shit, man. You just admitted you ain't got no gun. If that's so, how in hell did you wing him?"

"Yeah," said a hard voice to Longarm's left. "Explain that, mister!"

"Let me show you."

Carefully, Longarm reached into his vest pocket and pulled out his derringer; he had still not clipped it back onto the watch chain. "I said I didn't have a side arm. I didn't say I wasn't armed. I used this weapon."

A rider behind Longarm reached down and snatched the belly gun out of Longarm's hand, and holding it high, wheeled his horse around to face him. "You say you hit someone with this here pea shooter?"

"I'm not sure," Longarm replied patiently. "But I think so."

The Texan laughed derisively and tossed the tiny gun over his shoulder.

"Shit, Mac," another rider asked the trail boss, "what're we waitin' for?"

"That's right, Mac," another rider urged, "we're wasting time. I say string him up!"

6

When Longarm saw the trail boss about ready to give in to his men, he decided it was time to settle his identity before matters got any further out of hand. He had not wanted to reveal that he was a U.S. deputy marshal on assignment, not while he was this close to Pawnee Wells; but it was clear now that he had no choice in the matter. These Texans were on the prod and eager for hanging.

"Just hold up a minute," Longarm told the trail boss. "I think I have something here that will prove you've got the wrong man."

As Longarm spoke, he reached cautiously into his inside coat pocket for his wallet and the badge he kept in it.

"Hey! Watch out!" a rider cried. "He's goin' for another belly gun!"

The one with the rope dropped his loop over Longarm's head, turned his horse and lifted it to a gallop. Only by grabbing hold of the slip knot and preventing the noose from tightening about his windpipe was Longarm able to save himself. Racing along behind the rider, he cut behind a lone cottonwood and dollied the rope around the trunk. As the rope snapped taut against the saddle horn, the horse reared and sent the drover tumbling backward to the ground. Flinging the rope off his neck, Longarm rushed the downed rider, pulled the man's Colt from his holster and slammed it against the side of his head with enough force to knock him insensible.

The rest of the drovers were galloping after him. When they saw him knock the drover unconscious, they opened fire. Scrambling behind the trunk of a tall cottonwood, Longarm returned their fire. One drover cried out and peeled off his horse. Another grabbed his arm and turned his horse aside. The rest immediately veered away and continued to fire at him as they circled the tree, Indian fashion. Flat on the ground, Longarm poured fire at them until the Colt was empty. He broke it open and dug into his side pocket for fresh rounds and was exceedingly grateful to find that it accepted his .44-40 cartridges. The Texans, seeing him reloading, took this opportunity to tighten the circle, aiming more carefully now as they tried to finish him off.

One of the riders suddenly pulled up. It was too dark by this time for Longarm to see him clearly, and against the black line of the cottonwoods only the blaze running down his horse's face was visible. For some fool reason this rider had evidently decided he was the one to end this duel, and letting out an ear-splitting Comanche yell, he charged straight at Longarm. Fully reloaded by this time, Longarm steadied the Colt on a tuft of grass, sighted carefully on the horse's blaze, and squeezed the trigger.

The round carried high as Longarm had known it would and smacked into the rider's chest. He let out a muffled cry and flung his arms up as he toppled backward. The horse, riderless now, veered wildly and charged past Longarm. Infuriated, the rest of the drovers redoubled their rate of fire, a fusillade so intense Longarm was forced to keep his cheek plastered to the ground while the turf all around him began to churn like water boiling on a stove.

Abruptly, a rifle cracked from the trees behind the riders. One of the riders cried out and nearly toppled from his saddle as he yanked his horse around. Another rifle shot followed as the rest of the riders wheeled to meet this new, unexpected threat. A third shot cracked from the trees and this time a rider sprawled awkwardly forward over the neck of his horse.

"Hey!" one of the riders cried. "Jimmy's hurt bad!"

"I say we pull out!"

"Yeah! Let's get the hell out of here!"

"We can't!" a harsh voice insisted. "We got men down!"

"We'll have more men down if we don't get moving," the trail boss reminded them, turning his horse and heading back toward the stream.

"We can't ride off and leave this here rustler!"

"He's finished," another drover insisted. "He's down and he ain't movin'. No one could live through that fire."

Without joining the argument, Longarm continued to hug the ground. Another rifle shot cracked from the trees and Longarm heard the slug plow into a horse's spine and saw one of the horses drop as suddenly as if its legs had been cut off at the knees. The rider jumped clear and swung up behind another drover who, joining the fleeing trail boss, headed on a hard run for the stream. Wheeling their mounts, the rest of the Texans followed them into the line of trees. Longarm heard their horses charging across the shallow stream, and a moment later the pound of their hooves on the prairie beyond faded into silence.

Getting to his feet, Longarm heard a cricket in the trees near the stream. Then he heard the thud of a single horse's hooves and watched as a rider broke from the line of cottonwoods and rode toward him. The rider's upper body was in shadow, but Longarm didn't have to wait to know who it was. He could tell by the sight of his own Winchester resting across the pommel.

The breed had come back.

Chapter 2

"Who the hell *are* you, mister?" Longarm demanded.

"Some call me the Pawnee Kid."

"Why'd you come back?"

The Kid had ridden close enough now for Longarm to see the crooked smile on his face.

"Heard gunfire. Figured you could use some help."

"Saved by a horse thief," Longarm said dryly.

The Kid slipped the Winchester into the saddle scabbard and eased himself carefully out of the saddle. "I had me a damn good reason to keep right on ridin', and let them bastards fill you full of lead." He handed Longarm a slug pounded nearly flat. "This here's what I had to take out of my right side. Feels like it cracked one of my ribs. That's why I was still close by."

"Considering now what you were up against, I guess I can understand why you were so anxious to borrow my horse. I suppose I ought to thank you for coming back."

"If it hurts too much, you don't have to," the Kid drawled, handing Longarm his .44. "Don't need your .44 now, mister, or your hoss. You got a name?"

"My friends call me Longarm."

"You considering me a friend, are you?"

"You just saved my life. I figure that makes you a friend."

"Guess it does at that. You mind tellin' me what you're doin' out here. This is lonely country. Pawnee country."

"I'm a U.S. deputy marshal out of Denver. I got business in Pawnee Wells."

The Kid grinned and shook his head. "Gawdamighty! A U.S. marshal I picked to steal a horse from." He glanced over at the two riderless horses standing in the shadows near a stand of cottonwoods. "Anyway, looks like I got plenty of horseflesh to choose from now."

Longarm indicated the two downed Texans. "We better see about them two riders first."

They found the nearest Texan spread-eagled on his back, an astonished look on his face, his eyes staring glassily past them at the stars overhead. This was the one who had tried to hang Longarm. Remembering his sudden swipe downward with the Texan's own gun barrel, Longarm was astonished at the force his fury had generated; the blow had stove in the side of the drover's head, shattering it like an egg shell.

"I remember this bastard," said the Kid, squinting down at the dead man. "He's the one who strung up my partner, Tommy Black Eagle. Never saw a man so quick with a rope. Does my heart good to see him in this condition."

With the toe of his boot, Longarm nudged the dead man over onto his face. "He had a rope around my neck, too."

"You did real good gettin' away."

"I had some incentive."

The Kid stooped over the dead man to slip off his gun belt and holster. As he did so, Longarm left the Kid to walk over and examine the other drover. This one was as dead as the other one, crumpled on his side, a dark, gaping hole in his chest. A young man not much older than seventeen, he looked almost peaceful, the clean lines of his face soft in the dim starlight. Longarm felt a momentary qualm at the senseless waste of this young man's life.

Starting for the riderless horses, he skirted the dead one, and approached them carefully. The two spooked horses, a gray and a paint, stood trembling and uncertain close in to the cottonwoods. Talking low to calm them, he inched toward them. Once he was close enough, he patted their snouts for a second or two, then took their trailing reins. As he led them back across the flat to the Kid, he was lucky enough to spot his derringer gleaming dully in the grass. The dead man's gun belt sagging low on his hip, the Kid walked to meet him.

"Which horse do you want?" Longarm asked.

The Kid inspected the bigger one, a powerful chestnut, then pulled himself slowly into the saddle. It was obvious now that though the Kid had managed to extract the bullet from his wound, it was still pretty painful, especially if it had managed to crack a rib. The Kid patted the horse's neck and looked down at Longarm. "I'll take this one."

"You riding out now?"

The Kid glanced over at the two sprawled bodies. "I don't like the feel of this place. Too many dead spirits around."

"Don't seem right riding off without burying them two."

"You got a shovel?"

"Nope."

"And I'm hurtin'. If we dump 'em in the river, they'll only stink it up. Let them damn cowboys come back for their people."

"Well, I was going to camp here for the night. But I see what you mean, so I'm heading out too. Guess this is good-bye."

"Why so?"

"I told you. I'm on my way to Pawnee Wells."

"Hell, so am I."

"Let's go, then."

"You ain't gonna turn me in to the law when we get there, are you?"

"Nope, even though I got every reason and right to. Clubbing a federal marshal with his own gun and then stealing his horse ain't something the law takes lightly. Then again, I guess it's true you didn't know who I was when you did it, and like I said, if those hard cases were after me, I might have been tempted to do the same thing. And I figure I owe you something for coming back and saving my neck. But this is the end of it. After this we're even."

"It's all right by me. Let's ride."

Longarm mounted up and nudged his horse toward the stream. As they crossed it, the Kid managed to keep up, but once out on the prairie when Longarm lifted his mount to a lope, the Kid fell steadily behind. The hole in his side was obviously troubling him more than he was willing to admit. Longarm pulled his horse back down to a trot until the Kid caught up.

An hour or so after they put the stream behind them, they came upon a small pothole lake, a gleaming black saucer in the starlit night. When Longarm reached it, he reined in his mount and turned to the Kid.

"I'm done in. This is as good a place as any to camp."

Nodding wearily, the Kid eased himself off his horse. Longarm kept his head averted, then dismounted himself. He let the Kid unsaddle his horse while he picked out a spot to put down his bedroll. As he began to unroll it, the Kid dumped his own bedroll nearby and tried to get his own ready. Longarm saw the trouble he was having with the leather tie strings and without a word took over the chore. The Kid did not protest.

Later, as he slumped wearily back upon the blanket, Longarm said, "You better let me take a look at that wound."

"Don't worry. I already cauterized it. It's clean enough. Just sore is all. But I'd appreciate it if you'd help me bind up my ribs good and tight when we head out tomorrow morning."

"Sure."

"Hey. What's a federal marshal doin' headin' for Pawnee Wells?"

"That's for me to know, Kid, and no one else And when we ride in, I'd appreciate it if you didn't mention it until I get to see the sheriff."

"I won't say a word."

"You know the town?"

"I know it."

"You don't sound enthusiastic."

"Never did like townies."

"Any special reason?"

The Kid tipped his head, as if Longarm was kidding. "You mean you really don't know the reason? Look at me. I'm a half-breed, a stench in their white nostrils."

"You don't talk like an Indian."

"My ma took me from this country when my pa died, shot down by drunks who didn't think he had the right to ride into town with his head up and his shoulders back. I was a little shaver at the time. She took me all the way to Omaha. I got me a fine education there. I can read and write, which is more than a lot of these damned paleskins can do; but it don't make no difference with them. They see the Indian blood, and it raises their hackles." He grinned crookedly, his high cheekbones gleaming. "That's why old Pete had to lock me up so often."

The Kid's eyes closed then and his head dropped back onto his saddle. An instant later he was asleep. Reaching over, Longarm rested his hand lightly on the Kid's forehead and was pleased to find there was no fever. That derringer's bullet had sure slowed the Kid down some, but it would take more than that to stop him.

16

• • •

The prairie over which they had ridden for most of that day had been so flat that anything as tall as a tumbleweed or a prairie-dog mound seemed to loom as they approached it. Camping by another pothole lake that noon, Longarm had been able to glimpse under a patch of blue sky a horse and rider passing on the horizon at least a mile away.

And now, though Pawnee Wells was a good hour ride ahead of them, it was clearly visible, hanging spookily above the horizon. A pall of dust hung over it and Longarm could see a trail herd bedded down north of it. It was the Texans' cattle, Longarm guessed. Even though Pawnee Wells was not a railhead, trail herds and their drovers stopped there for a few days or so to replenish their chuck wagons and rest up in preparation for the Omaha stockyards.

Riding into town late that afternoon, Longarm could not help noticing the number of prosperous shops and warehouses lining both sides of the wide Main Street and the numerous alleys and bustling side streets branching off it. Pawnee Wells was prospering not only by supplying the sod busters moving onto the prairie, but from the business it managed to squeeze from the drovers passing through on one of the last remaining unfenced cattle trails, a feature that wouldn't last much longer. Barbed-wire fences were springing up everywhere; and the railroads were busy linking nearly every western town, striving to make it no longer necessary or even economical for cattlemen to drive their cattle to market on the hoof.

But until that day came, Pawnee Wells would welcome the business generated by every trail herd that passed by on its way to Omaha.

Riding down Main Street, Longarm's throat was as dry as gunpowder and the Kid was weaving slightly in his saddle, his face drawn; and on the Kid's suggestion, they nosed their mounts into the hitch rack in front of what appeared to be the town's largest saloon, the Golden Slipper. Longarm dismounted and waited patiently as the Kid took his time easing himself off his horse. As he stepped up onto the wooden sidewalk, he wobbled slightly. Seeing this, Longarm kept close beside him as they mounted the saloon's porch steps.

"Just get me to a table," the Kid told Longarm as they approached the batwings, "and bring me a drink. That'll fix me up just fine."

Longarm pushed through the batwings with the Kid, sighted an empty table against the wall and nodded at it to the Kid. As the Kid lurched almost drunkenly toward the table, Longarm pushed up to the bar and asked the barkeep for two glasses and a bottle of his best Maryland rye.

The barkeep slapped the bottle down, then deliberately placed a single glass beside it.

"I said two glasses," Longarm reminded him.

The barkeep glared balefully at Longarm and shook his head. "One glass is all you get, mister."

The barkeep was a large, round man with eyes resembling tiny raisins punched into a batch of bread dough. His oily hair was combed straight back, a neat part running down the middle of it. He wore a high starched collar that cut into the pendulous flap of flesh hanging from his chin.

"One glass?"

"That's right, mister."

"How come?"

"You ain't drinking in here with no half-breed."

For the first time Longarm became aware of how silent the saloon had become. He drew back slightly. "You want to explain that, mister?"

"We got rules in this town. We don't let no Indians or breeds drink in the same place as a white man."

"That so?"

The barkeep nodded stiffly, his small eyes flashing arrogantly. "You want the whiskey or don't you?"

Longarm stepped closer, reached out and grabbed the barkeep's starched collar, dragging him halfway over the counter. As the startled man snatched up the sawed-off shotgun he kept under the bar, Longarm brought the blade of his palm down on the man's wrist so hard the shotgun clattered down onto the bar's top. Turning his fist under the man's chin, he was pleased to see the man's unhealthy face grow slowly purple, his eyes start to bug. Longarm leaned his face close to the barkeep's.

"I'm going to let you go just as soon as you produce that other glass," he told the man. "You got that?"

Beads of perspiration streaming down his face, the barkeep managed a feeble nod and reached back under the bar, produced a second glass and set it clumsily down on the bar. Longarm let go of the barkeep's collar. The barkeep flopped back, dropping out of sight behind the bar, his strangled, gasping coughs filling the hushed saloon.

Picking up the bottle with one hand, the two glasses with the other, Longarm left the bar and walked over to the table where the Kid was waiting for him, his head resting forward on his crossed arms. He had apparently passed out. As Longarm sat down, a burly hard case, his right eye covered with a black eye patch, pushed himself out of the crowd of patrons staring at them and planted his feet wide, the palm of his right hand resting lightly on the walnut grips of his holstered Colt.

"We want you out of here, mister," the hard case said. "You and the Kid."

Longarm placed the bottle and two glasses carefully down on the table and poured himself a drink. The Kid, his head still resting on his forearms, did not move.

The man strode closer. "Damn your eyes, mister," he snarled. "You ain't dealin' with no fat barkeep now."

Longarm looked up at him. "No, I ain't, and that's a fact. I'm dealing with a prize asshole, looks like."

"Why, you—!"

Another man, squatter and bulkier than the one with the eye patch, stepped out of the encircling crowd of patrons and joined the other one.

"You heard Bud, mister. You ain't welcome in this town."

Downing his Maryland rye, Longarm leaned back, folded his arms, and smiled at the two men. "You two men calling us out?"

"That's right, Indian lover."

"Sorry. I got this bottle to finish."

"No, you ain't," the first man cried, his hand closing about his Colt.

Before he could bring it up all the way, Longarm leapt out of his chair and grabbed the man's wrist. Howling, he tried to pull free of Longarm's powerful grasp, but Longarm just continued to twist outward. The bone in the wrist snapped and with a sharp cry of pain the man dropped his gun. With his boot Longarm sent the gun skittering across the floor as the big man collapsed to the floor, whimpering, clutching at his wrist.

When Longarm turned then to deal with the other one, he saw him frozen in place, both hands in the air. Longarm glanced around to see the Kid, a wide grin on his face, covering the other one with the gun he had been keeping behind his crossed arms. He cocked it, the menacing sound echoing loudly in the hushed room.

"Go ahead, Dutch," the Kid urged softly. "Give me a reason to pull this trigger."

"Hell no, Kid," replied Dutch. "You got me cold, you have."

"Then get Gunther out of here. He's stinkin' up the place. He's liable to shit in his pants in another minute."

"Sure, Kid, sure," said Dutch.

He hurried over to Gunther and did his best to help the man to his feet. Still moaning, Gunther got to his feet, and still hanging on to his shattered wrist, followed Dutch from the saloon. He made no effort to pick up his Colt. The saloon's patrons, properly chastened, began to back away, their eyes averted, looking for all the world like rats hoping to find a hole into which they could crawl.

Longarm was sitting back down when a tall, handsome woman strode toward them. Just before she reached their table, she whirled to face the sullen crowd of patrons. In the withering glare of her contempt, they seemed to shrink visibly.

"I saw the whole thing from the balcony," she told

them, her furious gaze raking them. No one dared to meet her eyes. "Not a single one of you skunks lifted a hand to help this here stranger. No wonder Bud Gunther and Dutch Rawlings walk all over you men. You're all as yeller as fresh mustard and they know it. Go on," she concluded with icy contempt, "go on back to your vices. Far as I'm concerned, that's the only thing good about any single one of you."

As the men, properly chastised, slunk back to the roulette and poker tables, the woman turned and flung a withering, furious glance at the barkeep. "Sam, since when do you say who drinks in my saloon? You're finished here!"

"Finished?"

"You heard me. Get out. Now!"

With shaking hands, the barkeep untied his apron and dropped it onto the bar. "But Miss Virginia," he bleated, "what about my—"

"Come back at close tonight. I'll settle up with you then."

She turned then to face Longarm. "You all right, mister?"

"Sure," he said, grinning at her. "But I'm still thirsty."

She returned his smile and became suddenly very beautiful. "Drink up. That bottle of rye is on the house."

"Much obliged," said Longarm, immediately filling his and the Kid's glass.

"Hey, what's this, Virginia?" the Kid said, throwing down the rye. "You the sole owner of the Golden Slipper now?"

"That's right, Kid."

"What happened to Caulder?"

Virginia pulled out a chair and sat down at the table. "I learned how to cheat at cards, Kid. Then I saved my money and bought out Caulder. Right about now, I figure, he's somewhere between here and California."

"How about an introduction, Kid?" Longarm asked.

Virginia extended her hand. "The Kid ain't got no manners, mister. I'm Virginia Colbert."

"Custis Long," Longarm said, taking her hand. "Pleased to meet you."

"Kid," Virginia said, glancing back at him, "you don't look so hot."

"A little while back my friend here shot me."

Startled, Virginia glanced at Longarm.

Longarm shrugged. "It's the truth."

"But why?"

"He stole my horse."

"That's all right," the Kid explained to Virginia. "It was just an unfortunate misunderstanding."

"I'm not so sure, Kid. Seems like you're up to your old tricks. Rustlin' and now horse stealing. You keep on like this and you'll get your neck stretched."

Frowning, Longarm glanced at the Kid. During the ride that morning the Kid had assured Longarm that his troubles with the Texas drovers had begun when he and his trail buddy Tommy Black Eagle woke up to find a small herd grazing contentedly alongside the pothole lake where they had camped. Assuming the steers had strayed from a passing trail herd they had seen the day before, they had shrugged and gone about their morning toilet, intending to drive the herd back to the trail herd

23

later that day. They were still in the process of breaking camp when the Texans broke upon them without warning. While one of the Texans dropped a rope over the head of Tommy Black Eagle, the Kid had leaped on his horse and ridden off, MacDonald and the rest of the drovers in hot pursuit. When his horse foundered on the other side of the stream late that same day, the Kid was left afoot, and crossing the stream kept in the trees close to the bank until he came upon Longarm.

That had been the Kid's story, and it had gone far toward explaining to Longarm how the drovers had come to mistake him for the Kid. Since they had never managed to get very close to the Kid during their pursuit, they knew only that they were looking for an unarmed man afoot.

But now, with Virginia's remark echoing in his ears, Longarm found himself wondering once again how that stray bunch of cattle had managed to turn up at the Kid's encampment in the first place. Were MacDonald and his crew in the right after all? Had the Kid and Tommy Black Eagle rustled that gather of Texas cattle and then allowed themselves to be tracked to their campsite?

The Kid caught the doubt in Longarm's eyes. "Hey, Longarm!" he said. "Don't you pay no mind to Virginia here. I ain't no rustler. She likes to kid around. Ain't that right, Virginia?"

"Sure, Kid," Virginia said. "I'm just kidding around. By the way, where's Tommy Black Eagle?"

"Tommy's dead, Virginia. Some Texas drovers hung him. They looped a rope around his neck and dragged him until he was dead."

Virginia was shocked. "Jesus, Kid, I'm sorry. I didn't know."

"No way you could've known," the Kid said. "And it don't make me feel any better thinking about it."

"No wonder you look so awful."

"You going to put me up? I need some lovin' care." He managed a grin. "Is Annie still here?"

"She's here."

"Well now, that cheers me up some."

Virginia glanced at Longarm. "You need a place, too? You look about as done in as the Kid."

"I am that. What've you got in mind?"

"My apartment on the top floor."

"I wouldn't want to put you to any trouble."

"It's no trouble. There's plenty of room. Ask the Kid."

The Kid grinned and nodded. "She's right. There's plenty of room upstairs in this place. Many's the time Tommy and me hid out up there."

Longarm got up and helped the Kid to his feet. With Virginia leading the way, they pushed through the crush of men to a broad stairway at the rear and climbed past the second-floor cribs to the third-floor landing.

By the time they reached the doorway leading into Virginia's apartment, the Kid was so weak Longarm had to hold him up. His arm about the Kid's shoulder, he guided him inside, and with Virginia showing the way helped him into her bedroom. Pulling up beside the bed, Longarm turned the Kid around, then nudged him gently, and the Kid flopped loosely backward onto the bed. He was unconscious before the bedsprings stopped rocking. Virginia pulled off the Kid's boots and shooed

Longarm out of the room as she proceeded to undress him.

Taking out a cheroot, Longarm made himself comfortable on a sofa and lit up. He was almost finished with it when Virginia left the bedroom, excused herself as she hurried past Longarm, and opened the door to her apartment. She called down the stairs for someone, then stepped out into the hallway and pulled the door shut behind her as they conversed.

A moment later she returned to the apartment and joined Longarm, sitting down in an upholstered armchair across from him. For the first time Longarm got the chance to take her all in. Virginia Colbert was in the prime of her womanhood, with a waist he could have enclosed with both hands and a bust that swelled voluptuously under her emerald green bodice. Her complexion was fair, but not milk white, and her combed-out chestnut curls reached to her shoulders. Her manner and appearance radiated strength. Her nose was straight and uncompromising, her forehead broad, her mouth generous and full. She wore no cheek rouge or lipstick; she needed no such embellishments.

"How's the Kid?" Longarm asked.

"Asleep. I sent for the doc to take a look at his wound. But it isn't swollen too bad and doesn't look inflamed. He's just lost a lot of blood, I'm thinking."

"He's a tough kid."

"That he is."

"You known him long, Virginia?"

"Five years. Since the time he fell for a local hooker —fell hard, I might add."

"What happened?"

26

"He wanted to marry her. But she was too good for him. He's a breed, after all, and she was a white woman."

"How'd he take it?"

"I had to hold his hand for a while, but he came out of it all right. Tell me, Custis, how'd you happen to team up with him?"

Longarm told her, starting with his dip in the stream and ending with the Kid's sudden, very welcome reappearance. When he was done, she shook her head in admiration and wonder, a wry smile on her face.

"You mean the Kid came back to help you after you put that bullet in him?"

"That's the truth of it. And I'm glad he came back. Those Texans were getting meaner by the minute."

"They would've hung you, like they did Tommy Black Eagle. The Kid must feel pretty bad about Tommy. Them two've been riding together for as long as I can remember."

"Has this trail boss MacDonald and his crew shown up in your saloon yet?"

"No, but they're in town, sure enough—as mean as wet yellow jackets."

"We're lucky they didn't see us ride in."

"You won't be lucky for long. MacDonald and his crew will be here for a couple of days, at least. From what I heard, they got some provisions to buy and some heavy drinking to get done before they head for Omaha."

"The Kid better keep his tail down."

"That goes for you, too, now that you're sidin' the Kid."

"I can't hole up. I got business in this town that can't wait."

"Oh?"

"I'm looking for someone."

"Who?"

"Fellow called Pete Krueger."

"Why, hell, I know Pete. Everyone in town does. You won't have any trouble finding him. He lives across town in a one-bedroom shack with a whitewashed fence around it and a small garden and chicken house in back. He used to be the town marshal, and anytime you want to listen, he'll tell you all about the good old days when he stood up to Wyatt Earp and Doc Holliday and all the other mean gunslingers."

"Sounds like a real character."

"He is that."

"Can he be relied upon?"

"I'd say so, yes. Him and the Kid get along fine."

"I guess I'll go see him." Longarm got to his feet.

She walked with him to the door. "I'll keep an eye on the Kid."

Leaving the Golden Slipper a moment later, Longarm led his mount and the chestnut across the street to the livery, then headed for the sheriff's office. Striding into it, he found a deputy just pulling a cell door shut. A very drunk cowboy was sitting inside on the bunk, his head buried in his hands. He was moaning pitifully. Longarm thought he might be one of MacDonald's crew, but he couldn't be absolutely sure the way he was hunched over.

"Where's Sheriff Decker?" he asked the deputy.

"Who wants to know?"

The deputy was a tall drink of water, lean as a broom handle, sandy haired, with sky-blue eyes.

"My name's Custis Long. Where'd you say he was?"

The deputy dropped the keys onto his small desk in a corner and slumped down behind it into a straight-back wooden chair. He leaned the chair back against the wall and propped his feet up on the desk.

"I didn't."

"Well?"

Deciding the game was over, the deputy shrugged. "He's in Ma's restaurant across the street, eatin' his supper."

"I don't know the sheriff personally."

"Hell, you can't miss him. He's wearing a red vest with a polished star on it."

Without thanking the deputy, Longarm left the sheriff's office and crossed the street to the restaurant. Sheriff Ben Decker was seated alone at a table next to a window. His hat was off, revealing a thick shock of graying hair, a leathery roadmap of a face, and narrow, squinting eyes, the kind a man acquires after peering for too many years into blizzards, trail dust and hot sun. He looked up from his steak as Longarm halted by his table.

"Yeah?"

"Sheriff Ben Decker?"

"Last I heard, that was me, all right."

"Mind if I sit down?"

"I don't suppose there's anything I can do about it. Ordinarily, I don't conduct business when I'm eating."

"Sorry."

"Sorry don't help my digestion none."

Longarm dropped his hat on a tree by the table and sat down across from the sheriff. A waitress hurried over, and Longarm ordered a cup of coffee.

"I'm Custis Long, Sheriff. I work out of Billy Vail's office in Denver. He seemed to think you'd remember him."

The sheriff broke into a smile and pushed away his finished steak. "Why, sure I remember Billy. How is the old buzzard?"

"He's piling on some tallow around the middle, and there's less hair on top than when you knew him, I suspect."

Longarm's coffee arrived. He poured milk into it and shoveled in two teaspoons of sugar as the waitress put down a huge wedge of apple pie in front of the sheriff. His fork slicing into the pie, Decker glanced up at Longarm. "Who're you after, Deputy?"

"John Delsey, though I doubt he's going by that name now."

"You got a description of him?"

"He's in his early forties, about five ten, brown eyes, sandy hair, wore a mustache last time he was measured for a ball and chain."

His mouth full of apple pie, the sheriff snorted. "Hell's fire, Deputy. That description fits half the men in town. What's the poor bastard wanted for?"

"He likes to rob banks. Three years go he knocked off a bank in Kansas City and got away with two thousand worth of federal bank notes. That was what put him in the federal government's doghouse."

"What makes you think he's hiding out here in Pawnee Wells?"

"An informant."

The sheriff was making short work of the pie. "And who might that be?"

"Pete Krueger."

The sheriff cocked an eye at Longarm, then reached for his coffee to wash down the pie, almost choking in the process. "You crazy? *That* old buzzard?"

"Billy knows Pete. Said he was a pretty good sheriff until he quit a few years back. Billy said he's still a tough old bird."

"He may be tough, all right. Old meat usually is. But he's feedin' on loco weed these days. That crazy old duffer sees outlaws, desperadoes and crazed redskins under every bed. I hate to say this, Deputy, but you came a long way for nothin'."

"You'll have to let me be the judge of that, Sheriff."

"Sure. You go right ahead. But don't expect me to back you on that old fart's say-so."

Longarm got to his feet and reached for his hat. "I'd appreciate it if you'd keep this discussion confidential."

"Deputy, I won't be tellin' nobody. I'd be laughing too hard to get the words out."

As Longarm turned to leave, the sheriff cleared his throat. "Just a minute, Deputy..."

Longarm halted.

"Before you act on anything that old fool Pete tells you, I'm reminding you to check with me first."

"Check with you?"

Decker nodded curtly. "That's what I said, Deputy. This here ain't the Mile High City; this is my town, my jurisdiction. You'll keep me informed on all aspects of this case."

"Why, you stupid, officious son of a bitch," Longarm said with cold, quiet fury, "why in the hell do you think I stopped in here to watch you stuff your face in the first place, if it wasn't to keep you informed?"

In the act of picking up his cup of coffee, Decker's face went white as he let the cup clash back down onto its saucer. Nodding curtly, Longarm clapped his hat on, and strode from the restaurant. He would just have to own up to it: he had taken a mortal dislike to the local sheriff. Too bad. It could only make his assignment in this town that much more difficult to accomplish.

He heard a mean chuckle and glanced up to see two mounted riders staring at him. They were sitting their mounts just beyond the hitch rack, and as Longarm paused on the sidewalk both men drew their six-guns and leveled them on him.

"Hold it right there, mister," one of the drovers said.

"Yep," the other rider remarked to his companion, a pleased grin on his face. "You was right, Brazos. This here's the same dirty son of a bitch all right." He glanced down the street and shouted, "Over here, boys!"

Dismounting, the two cowboys strode up onto the sidewalk and halted in front of Longarm, legs spread, their big Colts still aimed at his gut. A third rider clattered up to the hitch rack. It was the trail boss.

"We knew you was in town, you bastard," he said, "when we saw a horse from my crew's string in the livery stable."

"The chestnut, you mean."

The trail boss nodded curtly and joined the two cowboys on the sidewalk. More of his crew rode up, dust kicking up around the porch as they slewed to a halt and dismounted. An eager crowd was gathering. From behind him, Longarm heard the restaurant door open and the tramp of heavy boots as someone strode out onto the restaurant's low porch.

"What's all this, Mac?"

Longarm recognized the sheriff's voice.

"We just caught ourselves a cattle rustler, Ben. We found him and his buddy bedded down alongside a gather of our stock they run off, and this one here killed two of my drovers."

"Two men killed, you say? Where are their bodies?"

"I've already sent men back for them."

"What you got to say about that, Long?" the sheriff asked, stepping off the porch and coming to a halt behind him.

Longarm glanced back at him. "It was self-defense."

"Self-defense, hell," said the trail boss. "We were only trying to bring you in for rustling."

"No, you weren't," said Longarm. "You were trying to hang me on the spot, the way you did Tommy Black Eagle."

"See that, Ben?" the trail boss said. "That's all the proof you need. He just identified his confederate, the redskin we strung up."

"He didn't string him up," Longarm said, looking back at the sheriff. "One of his crew roped him around the neck and dragged him until he was dead. They wanted to do the same thing to me. I ought to press charges myself. For attempted murder."

"Well, sir," the trail boss said, grinning at Longarm, "ain't you got sand. Pressing charges against me."

"You and your entire crew."

It was high time, Longarm figured, for the sheriff to bring this fool comedy to an end by revealing to the trail boss who Longarm was and what he was doing in Pawnee Wells. After all, it would be clearly indisputable that a deputy marshal out of Denver was hardly likely to be in league with local rustlers.

Instead, the sheriff asked the trail boss, "What do you want me to do with him, Mac?"

"Ben," the man said reasonably, "I already told you what he done. He rustled my cattle and killed two of my crew. And stole a Circle Bob horse. Tell you what. Lock him up till I get back from Omaha. I want to see this bastard swing from a gallows."

"Damn you, Sheriff," Longarm said, "tell this man who I am."

"You mean who you say you are."

Before Longarm could argue further, he felt the bore of the sheriff's six-gun digging cruelly into the small of his back. Longarm swung around to face him. Chuckling meanly, the sheriff shoved the Colt still deeper.

"Steady there now, Mr. Long. You give me trouble, start resisting arrest, there won't be no need for a hanging. We'll settle matters here in front of all these witnesses."

As he spoke, he reached under Longarm's coattail and lifted his .44 out of his cross-draw rig. Then, prodding Longarm energetically with his six-gun, he propelled him through the grim ring of cowpokes and out into the street. As he reached the jail house, Longarm told himself that the sheriff had only Longarm's best interests at heart; he was going along with the trail boss's crazy charges that he was a horse thief and rustler only in order to get Longarm out of the grasp of this irate crew of Texans.

The trouble was, Longarm had a great deal of difficulty believing this.

Chapter 3

The six-gun still jammed into his back, Longarm entered the sheriff's office and waited for Decker to put away the gun. When he didn't, when he continued to shove Longarm toward a cell, Longarm spun angrily around and slapped the man's gun down.

Decker took a step back and swung his Colt, catching Longarm on the side of his head. The blow staggered him, and as he rocked back, groping for something to hang on to, the deputy caught him from behind and pinned his arms. Decker stepped close, reached into Longarm's inside coat pocket and lifted out his wallet, then his watch and derringer, after which the deputy spun him into a waiting cell. Longarm hit the cot hard, his head slamming into the wall. Grinning, the deputy turned the key in the lock.

Longarm was furious. "Goddamn it, Decker, what the hell's the matter with you?"

Decker stepped close to the cell and peered in through the bars at Longarm. "You already spelled that out yourself, Deputy. I'm a stupid, officious son of a bitch. Don't you remember?"

"Well, if you believe that trail boss's account of what happened out there, you're even more stupid than I thought."

"Listen, Deputy, why shouldn't I believe MacDonald? You didn't tell me nothin' about this run-in with MacDonald and his crew, let alone them two dead men. Why not?"

"That's my business."

"Well, keepin' the peace in this town's my business. And MacDonald's got witnesses, his whole damn crew. And all I got from you is your charge that MacDonald and the rest of them are liars."

"What's that supposed to mean, Decker? You know goddamn well I didn't come all the way from Denver to rustle that fool's cattle."

"Maybe not. But I'll bet even money you know who did. Who're you covering for, Deputy? I been hearin' things. Like the Kid's back in town. Rode in with a tall drink of water, yourself as a matter of fact."

"That's beside the point. You know MacDonald's charges are crazy."

The sheriff chuckled meanly. "Maybe so, Deputy. But you got to understand my side of it. I work for this county, but mostly for this town, and the merchants in this town know which side their bread is buttered on. Right now, these free-spending Texas drovers are mighty welcome. So locking you up is the wisest course for everyone concerned."

"And that's why you're letting MacDonald get away with this?"

"Try to see it our way. What's good for business is good for the town."

"Which means MacDonald and his crew are now calling the shots."

"For now, yes."

"How long you plan keeping me in here?"

"Until MacDonald and his riders sober up and move out for Omaha."

"You're forgetting something. MacDonald expects to return for my trial."

"Sure he does, now. But once he sells his beef in Omaha and pays off his crew, he'll be on the first train for Texas. And even if he does come back like he said he would, I'll just tell him you made bail and lit out."

"I'd rather you let me out now, Sheriff. I'd prefer to take my own chances with those drovers."

"That wouldn't be wise, Deputy. We'll do it my way."

Longarm leaned back against the wall and studied the sheriff. He did not trust the man. But at the moment, it seemed, he had no choice but to go along and see what developed.

The sheriff turned and strode past his deputy and out the jail house door.

Slumping back full length on his bunk, Longarm crossed his arms under his head and stared up at the ceiling. Soon, as night fell, his ears picked up through the open window above his bunk the sounds of a trail town at night. Heavy, booming laughter. The rapid tinkle of honky-tonk pianos swelling out through batwing doors. The shrill squeal and sudden, clear laughter of good-time gals being pinched and fondled. And every now and then came the sudden pound of horses' hooves as fresh drovers rode into town, some of them punctuating their arrival with gunfire.

What he heard underlined the truth of the sheriff's assertion that the town welcomed and needed the business these drovers brought to it. Nevertheless, Longarm had a nagging suspicion that there was more to the sheriff's willingness to incarcerate him than placating MacDonald and his crew.

The deputy strode over to the cell door and peered in at him, a grin on his face. "If you're hopin' for supper, mister, forget it. You're too late."

"What's your name, friend?"

"Frank. Frank Carson."

"Well, Frank, thanks for the good word."

Longarm made himself as comfortable as he could on the wooden bunk and closed his eyes. He hadn't slept since the night before and the ride to Pawnee Wells had been a long one, so long that the hard bunk almost seemed to cradle him like a mother's arms as he fell almost immediately asleep.

Longarm awakened with the roar of a distant crowd in his ears. Sitting up on the bunk he scratched his head and glanced through the bars. The sheriff's office was empty. The deputy was gone, the only light coming from a single lamp on a table. Longarm got the distinct feeling that he had been abandoned.

"Longarm!"

It was the Kid. He was calling to him from the alley below the cell's open window. Standing up on the bunk, Longarm peered out through the bars but could see only a privy's dim, leaning shape in the alley below. A rock suddenly struck the bars and bounced back out. He went up on tiptoes, and peering almost straight down he saw the Kid standing beside his horse under the window, a rope in his hand.

"What the hell are you trying to do, Kid?"

"Can't you hear that crowd? MacDonald and his crew are fixin' to lynch you, and most of the town is eager to help."

"Where's the sheriff?"

"Forget him. And his deputy. From what I hear, they ain't about to do anything to discourage this here neck-tie party. Here! Grab this rope and tie it around the bars."

The Kid swung the rope around his head, then let go. A rock tied to the end of it pulled the rope up through the bars after it. Longarm grabbed it, untied the rock, then knotted the rope securely around the bars.

"Done!" he cried, stepping back off the bunk.

He heard the Kid mounting his horse, heard its hooves digging into the alley floor. The rope grew suddenly taut. A muffled shout to his mount came from the Kid and the bars began to pull loose. The pressure on the bars increased and suddenly they broke free of the sill and were dragged out through the window.

Longarm flung his hat out ahead of him, then stuck his head through the opening and climbed out, dropping

41

lightly to the ground. He picked up his hat and untied the rope from around the window bars.

The Kid rode back to him. "Let me have your hat and coat," he said.

"Why?"

"You ask too many questions."

The lynch crowd was closer now. Longarm could hear the men marching down the middle of the street. Shrill cries and mean-spirited shouts were met with wild, approving laughter. Everyone was looking forward to a good time and it would not be long before members of the crowd would be close enough to charge into the jail to drag their victim out. Already, the gloom on the other side of the jail was growing lighter from the glow of many torches.

Without further argument, Longarm handed his Stetson up to the Kid, and shrugging out of his frock coat let the Kid have that as well. In exchange, the Kid dropped his sheepskin jacket to Longarm and handed him his own straight-brimmed Stetson.

"Virginia's waitin' back at the Golden Slipper," the Kid told him. "Don't go in the front way. She'll be in the alley by the back door." As he spoke, he tucked his black hair up under Longarm's hat, then tugged the brim down to hide as much of his face as he could.

"What the hell are you up to, Kid?"

"Watch!"

Wheeling his horse, the Kid cut up the alley beside the jail house and bolted out onto the main street. As soon as the mob saw the Kid ride out of the alley wearing Longarm's hat and coat, they let out a roar of pure frustration, the howl of a famished beast denied its red meat.

"There he goes!" someone cried. "The son of a bitch is getting away!"

At once came the cries for men to get their horses, and it was not long before a posse of angry horsemen clattered out of town, hot on the Kid's tail. Crouching in the near pitch-black darkness of the alley, Longarm waited until the last of the horsemen had left town and the disheartened remnants of the lynch mob had dispersed. Once he judged it was safe to do so, he entered the jail through the back door. Walking over to the sheriff's desk, he retrieved his derringer and watch, took back his wallet and badge, then went over to the table to pick up his .44. Dropping it into his cross-draw rig, he ducked back out into the alley and headed for the Golden Slipper. He had not gone far when a shadowy figure stepped out of an alley doorway.

"Hey, Kid. Where the hell're you goin'?"

Longarm recognized Frank Carson's voice. The deputy was not close enough to see Longarm's face, only the Kid's familiar hat and sheepskin coat. Without replying to the deputy's query, Longarm kept his mouth shut and his head down as he continued to stride toward him.

He was within a few feet of Carson when he heard the deputy mutter, "Hey! You ain't the Kid!"

"That's right, asshole."

As Carson's hand dropped to his six-gun, Longarm lunged at him. His head slammed into Carson's chest, ramming him back into the doorway. Clamping his left hand down on Carson's wrist, Longarm sealed the deputy's revolver in its holster. At the same time, keeping his right arm bent, he rammed his elbow into Carson's face with a savage, full-bodied blow that wedged his head between the door and the frame, the full weight of his body pinning Carson into it. In an effort to free the revolver from its holster, Carson tugged desperately on his gun butt. Easing up slightly, Longarm let him lift out the gun. As soon as the revolver cleared leather, Longarm swept down with his right hand, batting the gun out of Carson's hand. It thudded heavily to the alley floor, and with one thrust of his foot Longarm sent it spinning across the alley.

Carson braced his foot against the door frame, lowered his head, and drove as hard as he could at Longarm, his head crunching against Longarm's shoulder, nudging him back. Continuing the pressure, Carson drove Longarm back. Longarm abruptly lost his balance, but held on to Carson's wrist with his left hand, and falling, pulled him out of the doorway. Using his falling weight as a lever, he yanked hard on Carson's arm, propelling the deputy past him in a staggering, off-balance lunge. Longarm's back hit the alley floor with a crunch that drove the breath from him in a deep grunt.

Rolling over, he saw Carson struggling to regain his feet. Hurling himself at the deputy, Longarm smashed him flat, then hauled the deputy upright and drove a solid blow into his midriff and heard the sharp explosion of breath that followed. Wrapping both arms around his gut, Carson doubled over. Longarm moved a half-step to the right, then drove his right fist flush against the side of the deputy's face. The force of the blow spun

Carson half around. He staggered and seemed ready to collapse.

Longarm stepped close then, intending to finish Carson off. But Carson was game. As he spun around, he kicked out with his foot and managed to catch Longarm's left knee, collapsing the leg under him. Longarm pitched clumsily sideways to the ground. As he rolled over to push himself upright, another kick knifed into his side. Despite the pain rocking through his ribs, Longarm struggled upright. Close to complete exhaustion, Carson had rocked back and was clinging to the post of a back porch. Longarm could hear his great, shuddering inhalations as the man struggled to suck air into his lungs.

Testing his left leg, Longarm found it would hold his weight. Determined to end the grim contest once and for all, he moved quickly in on the exhausted Carson, and with a rapid series of sledging blows pounded him about his head and shoulders, each blow rocking Carson back deeper into the shadows until his back was hard against a wall. But Carson fought back stubbornly, managing to ward off and parry Longarm's merciless battering; but with a steady, dogged, killer stubbornness, Longarm continued to slash at him. Those of Carson's counterpunches he couldn't check or parry, he accepted silently and with head down, shoulders hunched, and kept on slugging, determined to break through the man's guard.

At last Carson's arms, unable to take the punishment, lowered slightly. Instantly Longarm closed in and hooked a hard right to the deputy's jaw that drove his head back against the wall. With cold, deadly precision

Longarm began sledging blow after blow into the man's face. Carson's knees buckled and he sagged forward. Longarm stepped back, letting Carson crumple to the ground.

His own breath coming in short gasps, each inhalation causing a spike of pain to erupt in his chest, Longarm looked wearily up and down the alley to make sure no one had heard or seen the quick, violent battle and was coming to investigate. Apparently no one had. Stepping back again from the downed Carson, Longarm picked up his hat, turned, and continued on down the alley.

A grunt from behind alerted him, but before he could react a force drove into his back with a savage thrust, driving him to his knees. Carson's arm dropped over his face and tightened against his gullet while his other arm drove past the opened coat and plunged a knife into Longarm's chest. The blade seared along a rib and then buried itself deep.

Through that pain Longarm acted instinctively. Holding Carson's arm and hand clamped tight against his chest, he humped his back and dove head foremost to the ground. As his head made contact, he felt Carson sail over his back. Still hanging on to Carson's arm, he felt it straighten with the weight of Carson's body pulling against it. Leaning over farther onto Carson's arm, Longarm heard as well as felt the elbow snap sickeningly under his weight. Carson shrieked in pain. Longarm let go and, still on his hands and knees, pulled the knife out of his side and flung it away, feeling as he did so the hot warm stream of fresh blood gushing out after it. Carson, mewling piteously, writhed on the alley floor, his forearm hanging at an odd angle from his elbow.

Longarm lurched upright, snatching up the Kid's hat again as he did so, and ran crookedly on down the alley, pain searing his entire right side. When he reached the block across the street from the Golden Slipper, he pulled his brim down over his face and strode quickly out of the alley and across the street. He staggered for a moment as he approached the saloon, but at that time of night the sight of a man under the influence seemed perfectly normal; no one paid him any attention as he lurched into the alley alongside the Golden Slipper. Turning the corner he saw Virginia waiting in the shadow of the saloon's back door.

"Hurry!" she cried, pulling open the door. Her long white nightdress gave her a ghostly appearance in the gloom of the alley.

Inside, Longarm took one look at the flight of stairs he would have to negotiate and halted to get his breath.

"What's the matter?" Virginia asked.

"I've been knifed."

"Oh, my God," she breathed, taking his left arm. "Let me help."

"I'd appreciate it."

With Virginia helping him, Longarm made it almost to the third floor before passing out. Not until she and two of her bar girls had managed to lug his long frame into Virginia's bedroom and dump him onto her bed did he regain consciousness.

"Go easy there," he murmured, winking at one of the girls.

"Does it hurt very much?" Virginia asked anxiously, pulling off his boots.

"It hurts enough."

She helped him take off the sheepskin jacket and gasped at the blood-soaked shirt she found underneath. After she had peeled that and his undershirt off, she inspected the raw wound closely, then left the room. Moments later she hurried back in with an armload of towels, one of her girls following in behind her carrying a pan containing a steaming solution of carbolic acid and water, the pungent smell of which filled the room.

Folding one of the towels into a compress, she soaked it in the antiseptic solution and held it firmly against the wound to staunch the flow of blood. It took two more such compresses to do the job, and with that done she bound the wound tightly. The bar girl gathered up the bloody bandages, along with his blood-soaked shirt and undershirt, and left the room.

Longarm leaned back against a pillow Virginia had propped against the headboard.

"How do you feel now?" Virginia asked.

"Better, thanks."

"You'd better go easy now. You lost a lot of blood."

"I'm sorry to cause all this trouble."

"Forget it."

"The Kid's got that bum side. He shouldn't have taken such a chance to spring me like that."

"He felt . . . responsible."

Longarm looked closely at her. "The Kid and Tommy Black Eagle were rustling MacDonald's cattle, weren't they?"

She hesitated only a moment, then nodded. "I don't

suppose it'd do any good to lie to you. And I'm sure the Kid intended to level with you sooner or later. The Kid has always been a wild one. Him and Tommy."

"Apparently that never stopped you from helping them."

"Like the Kid, I got no love for most of the men in this town. They're an unholy pride of damn fools and hypocritical bastards. Sure, they're willing to use me and my girls when their appetites take them, but in the cold light of day, they treat us like dirt." She smiled ruefully. "You might say the Kid and I, as fellow outcasts, saw no reason not to stick together."

"How'd you get wind of the lynching?"

"Some of the girls heard MacDonald and his crew tanking up, bragging about how far they were going to stretch your neck. They didn't seem to have any trouble at all swelling their ranks with townsmen." She shuddered at the thought. "Hell, when their guts are full of cheap liquor, there's nothing them turds like better than a good lynching."

"And the cheap liquor you provide."

She sighed, shrugging ruefully. "Ain't it the truth."

A sudden, drugged weariness threatened to overwhelm Longarm. He felt as if he had just been poleaxed as his eyelids became as heavy as anvils. Seeing how close he was to passing out, Virginia pressed him gently back into the pillows, covered him with a fresh blanket and stepped back.

"Get some sleep now," she told him softly.

Longarm barely managed a nod to her as he closed his eyes and spun off into a deep, exhausted sleep, the last image flashing across his mind that of the Kid gal-

49

loping out of town, a howling pack of horsemen hard on his heels.

Earlier, as soon as the Kid had put the town behind him and was well out onto the prairie, he turned his horse and made for the trail herd bedded down north of the town. He was within a couple of miles of it, the sound of pursuit growing louder behind him, when his horse snapped its leg in a gopher hole and went down hard. The Kid tumbled forward over the horse's neck, skidded a few yards on the damp grass, leaped to his feet and started running. He was still a good mile from the herd when he looked back and saw the pursuing riders looming out of the night less than a hundred yards back. They were closing fast.

He flung himself to the ground, rolled over and kept rolling to his right until he felt himself drop into a slight depression. There he remained. His gunshot wound had been torn open when he was flung off the horse, and the long run afterward had not helped any. A scalding pain pulsed in his side, but it was nothing compared to what he would suffer if he let any of these cowboys take him. Flat on his back, his gun out, he waited as the ground around him began to shudder from the pound of onrushing hooves.

"His horse's down!" a townsman cried out. It was a voice the Kid vaguely remembered.

"Where?"

"Over there!"

"I saw him!" another one called out. "He ran over there! I think he's down!"

The Kid felt as well as heard the horses converging

on him; cocking his revolver, he aimed it straight up. A huge dark body pounded close by on his right. Another swept past on his left even closer; damp clods of dirt struck the side of his face. He heard a horse behind him swerve slightly and, glancing straight up, saw its shod hooves clearing his body, then biting the ground inches beyond his boots. It swept on without pause, the rider not looking back.

In a moment his pursuers had surged on past him and the Kid started to breathe again. He waited for the pound of hooves to fade, then got to his feet to peer after them.

"Hey!" came a surprised voice behind him. "Here he is!"

The Kid whirled to see a lone horseman bearing down on him. In the dim starlight the Kid recognized him as the swamper who worked for one of the saloons in town. He was not wearing a hat and his sandy hair was wild as he pounded toward the Kid brandishing a huge Navy Colt.

"Hey, fellers!" he cried again. "He's back here!"

But it was too far for his shout to reach them, and the poor son of a bitch did not realize that it was now just between him and the Kid. Only the two of them. Sawing on the reins of his horse, he pulled to one side and managed to get off a shot at the Kid. The slug went wild. Dropping to one knee, the Kid fired back. Hit, the swamper yanked back on his horse's reins, causing the horse to rear wildly, its front hooves pawing at the sky. The swamper tumbled backward off the horse. Racing over, the Kid saw that he had caught the swamper in the shoulder. He was lying facedown, groaning. The Kid smashed him on the back of the head with his Colt, silencing him. Then he walked over to the horse, grabbed its reins and swung into the saddle.

The two gunshots had already alerted the riders, and as the Kid headed once again for the trail herd, he saw a string of riders peeling back toward him. But the Kid had too much of a lead on them. Head low over the neck of his horse he reached the edge of the cattle well ahead of his pursuers, took out his Colt and began punching the night sky with hot lead.

Already on their feet at the sound of the Kid's approach, the herd turned as one and bolted, the thunder of their pounding hooves filling the night. Sweeping to their rear and still firing over their heads, the Kid turned them toward the town, then kept after them, gaining slightly on them as they reached the town's outskirts. Through the back alleys they bulled their way, flooding like a horned river onto Main Street, a swift, bleating tide of destruction smashing away porches, plunging through store windows, knocking over lampposts; the few townsmen still about this late ran for cover, some dashing through windows in their haste to escape. Others kicked open locked doors, while still others shimmied up porch posts to escape the torrent of maddened brutes sweeping under them.

Once in the town, the Kid leaped off his horse and broke for cover, diving under a porch a few seconds before a furious band of weary, cursing riders charged past him down an alley, and found themselves caught up in the stampeding herd.

• • •

Longarm sat bolt upright in his bed. The room was shaking, as was his bed. A bone-deep thunder seemed to fill the universe. At that moment Virginia pushed through the door and hurried past his bed to the window.

"It's a stampede!" she cried, pushing aside the curtains to look down. "The streets are filled with cattle!"

Longarm flung back the blanket covering him and got out of bed. His head swam for a moment but he caught hold of a bedpost, steadied himself, then joined Virginia at the window.

Watching the dark, tumultous sweep of horns and backs wriggling and bawling through the narrow streets, Longarm grinned.

"It's the Kid," he told Virginia. "He's the one who stampeded these cattle."

"But why?"

"To get back into town and find a place to keep his ass down. There's sure as hell no place to hide out there on that prairie."

In a hushed voice, her eyes following the awesomely destructive trail left by the stampeding animals below her, she asked, "Do you really think so?"

"How often do those trail herds invade Pawnee Wells?"

"This is the first time that I know of."

"There's your answer."

She turned then to look at him, and gasped in surprise.

Longarm looked down and saw that he was standing before her stark naked. He grinned ruefully.

53

"You took off my clothes. Remember?"

"Of course I remember," she replied, a devilish look gleaming in her eyes. "You just . . . surprised me, is all. Maybe you better get back in bed. You haven't slept long and you're still a very weak man."

"Is that how I look?"

Laughing softly, she gently turned him around and guided him back to her bed. She was wearing a satin rose-colored robe and her dark, lustrous hair had been combed out so that it flowed halfway down her back in one solid, gleaming wave.

"Where were you sleeping?" he asked her.

"I just dropped off on the couch."

"Sleep in here then. I'll take the couch."

"No. We'll compromise." She smiled wickedly. "We'll both sleep in here."

He returned to the bed and slumped woozily back down on it as she drew the covers over him. He watched her move around to the other side, slip out of her robe, and throw back the sheets before climbing in. The sleeping gown she wore under her robe was nothing more than a long white silk man's shirt.

"I'm not promising anything," he told her.

"I wouldn't expect you to, not in your condition. I mean, after what you've just been through."

He watched her get into the bed, her shirttails riding up, affording him a quick glimpse of her pubic triangle against a flash of thigh. As she pulled the covers up over her, she cocked an eyebrow at him.

"But don't forget. Tomorrow's another day."

"I tell you what," he said. "Wake me early."

54

A moment later as she snuggled close to him, he felt her warm hand resting on his thigh and realized just how she planned to wake him. With the sound of the stampeding cattle fading in his ears and a smile on his face, he dropped back to sleep.

Chapter 4

The Pawnee Kid awoke at dawn. The bleeding had
stopped, but his wound was as sore as a bad tooth.
Rolling out from under the porch, he dusted himself off
and looked around. The alley was empty and he saw no
one passing on Main Street. He walked through the
alley to it and peered up and down. The town was quiet,
very quiet, even for this hour. The light grew better and
he found himself chuckling at the shattered plate glass
windows, the one flattened lamppost, and the damaged
porches, some of them with their support posts hanging
loosely from the porch roofs. At the end of the street, he
glimpsed what was left of a porch that had been swept
into the middle of the street. The carcass of one steer lay
half in and half out of a store window where some infuriated townsman had caught up to the frenzied beast
and shot it.

He knew then why it was so quiet. Those that could ride were off helping the drovers round up their scattered cattle, a chore the Kid knew would take some time. Everyone else was so stunned by the stampede and so filled with rotgut whiskey, they were too hung over and disheartened to open up their stores and begin to repair the damage.

His first thought was to return to the Golden Slipper and see if Longarm had made it back to Virginia's apartment all right. The trouble was he was now on the opposite end of town, which meant he had a long way to go to get there. His wound had opened up considerably now and he was losing blood. He didn't want to punish himself any more than he had to. He thought then of old Pete. His place was just over one block, and the Kid might be a lot better off bunking with him for a while. It wouldn't be the first time he had sought refuge with the old lawman.

The Kid reentered the alley and headed for Krueger's place.

When the Kid was a lot younger, he hadn't always got along with Pete Krueger, even though he always respected the lawman. Over the years since Pete unpinned his star, he and the Kid had managed to forge a pretty decent friendship, even though at times the old ex-lawman lost his patience with some of the Kid's escapades. Now, as the Kid saw Pete's small house on the corner ahead of him, he began to rehearse how much he should tell Pete this time.

Pete's rooster was crowing halfheartedly in the backyard as the Kid stepped over the low whitewashed picket fence in the front of the place. He mounted the low porch and knocked loudly on the door, assuming it would take something extra to rouse the old man this early.

There was no answer so he knocked again, louder.

The door sagged open.

"Pete . . . ?" the Kid called, pushing the door open all the way and stepping inside. "Ain't you up yet?"

When there was no response, the Kid headed for the bedroom, wondering if the old coot had been crazy enough to ride off with the others to help round up MacDonald's steers.

Pushing open the bedroom door, he heard the chink of spurs behind him and started to turn, but before he could turn around all the way, the roof collapsed onto his head and he pitched forward into darkness.

His mind foggy with sleep, Longarm became aware of Virginia's naked body easing onto his, the lush incandescence of her body igniting him clear down to his crotch. He opened his eyes and saw her face inches from his, a wicked smile on her face. She leaned still closer, her mouth parting, the musky smell of her hair cascading down over his head and shoulders adding the final, intoxicating element.

"You told me to wake you up early, Custis."

"Yes, I did."

"This should do it then."

She closed her thighs around his waist and eased herself back onto him, her moist pubis nudging against his growing erection. Her lips closed about his then, her tongue probing deeply, wantonly. He felt himself roaring to life. And so did she. She leaned back onto him and let her hot muff swallow his erection. Reaching up, he cupped both her breasts with his hands, their incredible warmth transmitting itself through his palms.

"Mmm," she said, rocking back and forth, her head flung back.

He tightened his hands on her breasts and heard her sigh of pleasure; she leaned forward and kissed him again, her mouth working furiously, hungrily. Pulling back, she looked searchingly into his face.

"Are you sure you are not too tired for this?"

"Shut up and get on with it."

"I don't wish to cause you pain."

"You will if you don't continue. All I can feel is that lovely muff of yours closing on me."

She laughed softly. "Like this, you mean?"

Her vagina closed about his penis like a fist. He groaned with the pleasure of it and reaching down, caught her hipbones and planted her still further down onto him. Abruptly, unable to contain his urgent need, he rolled over onto her, keeping himself still inside her as he did so, then thrusting down savagely as soon as he was atop her.

"Yes, yes, yes!" she told him fiercely, her face a mask of concentration; she began to fling her head from side to side with each answering thrust of her own.

He plunged deeper each time, it seemed, while she sucked him in still further, drawing in her breath in deep, ragged gasps. Her hands slid rapidly, frantically up and down his back, her nails raking him. By this time he had forgotten all about his wound, though he was aware of it protesting with every movement he made; it was as if the pain belonged to someone else.

60

Their manic frenzy increased until it became something as basic and as elemental as a cloudburst lashing a mountainside. Or the titanic crash of thunder, the ripping tear of a lightning flash.

Sharp, tiny cries came from Virginia as their bodies slapped wildly against each other in a rapidly accelerating crescendo. Too soon it was over. He heard Virginia cry out and felt her shuddering violently under him. He was carried over the crest then himself as a series of involuntary spasms left him so weak, so spent, he could barely pull free and roll off her wet, gleaming body.

"Wasn't that lovely," she murmured.

"Yes," he replied, panting.

"Are you awake now?" she asked.

He chuckled. "Wide awake."

Turning to face her, he winked at her and let one arm rest on her silken hip, the musky smell of their lovemaking filling the bedroom. Outside, the morning was getting steadily brighter and he could see even more clearly her dark, glowing eyes. They were intent, watching him closely, probing.

"Are you finished?" she whispered softly. "I mean completely finished?"

"Why're you asking?"

"I don't want to make your wound any worse."

"What wound? I don't feel a thing."

"I don't believe you."

"Trust me."

"All right," she said. "I'll trust you."

She leaned her face close and he kissed her, not on the lips, but on the neck under her ear. She sighed and he gently moved his lips up to tongue her earlobe. The searing intensity of a moment before was gone, replaced now by a need to caress and be gentle, to feel her open before him like a flower to the sun. He became aware of passion building slowly within him again. He let his hand explore the warmth of her sumptuous breasts, his fingers flicking the upraised nipples delicately. She let her head fall back on the pillow as she stirred her long legs lasciviously. She sighed softly.

` "Oh, yes," she murmured. "That's nice, very nice."

He saw that her face was flushed and heard her breath coming in short tiny gasps. Only then did he lean close and close his lips about hers. They softened eagerly, opening for his probing tongue, the sweet scent of her coming to him, stronger, much stronger even, than before. Her hands had already found his reviving erection. Feverishly, she stroked him back to a thrusting, urgent rigidity.

Grabbing her hip, he pulled her hard against him. With no further hesitation, she raised her leg for him inviting his entrance. He thrust easily, gently into her, then flowed over onto her once again, probing deep into her fiery sheath. Her eyes clamped shut, she panted eagerly, closing her thighs, sucking him in deeper. Easing himself up onto his knees, he ignored the protest of his knife wound and straddled her hips, going slowly wild with the feel of her inner muscles tightening on him deep inside her.

Then she began to move again, this time with a slow, expert rotation of her hips. Leaning well back, she heaved herself upright so that her heels could dig into his back. Intent now, both of them contemplating nothing but their mounting urgency, they struggled against each other.

"Go deeper, Custis! Deeper!"

Her aching urgency was as desperate as his. His previous gentleness he discarded now and he lunged into her savagely, fiercely, exulting as he saw a flush darken her face. She flung her head back, grunting deeply with each thrust. He grasped her breast and squeezed, feeling her firm nipple react to his insistent caresses. From deep within her a sharp cry broke as she heaved her pelvis up at him. Fighting her, he slammed her back down with all his might, driving deep, impaling her on the bed, the force of it causing the air to explode from her lungs. Grinning up at him, she huffed with each plunge, meeting each of his thrusts eagerly, her face shining with perspiration. Faster and faster, wilder and wilder, he plunged, reaching far back, aware that he was approaching a crest. Then he was beyond it, bursting over, flooding Virginia for the second time in his spasming copulation as she clung to him fiercely, gyrating wildly under him as she too climaxed, gasping with each shuddering spasm.

At the end of it, spent completely, as empty as a rain barrel in August, Longarm sagged forward onto her, his huge frame meshing with her lush peaks and valleys, dimly aware of her pleased, wondering exhalation as she wrapped her arms and thighs about him, binding him to her. For a long, delicious while they lay in each other's embrace, allowing the glow of their coupling to fade at its own sweet leisure, unwilling to hurry it.

At last, gently, pulling free of her and rolling onto

his side, he propped his face on his elbow and smiled at her.

"That last time," he said, "you were not putting on a performance."

She laughed, a low, seductive sound, and reached her hand out to his. "I assure you, Longarm. Not that last time."

"Good."

"You must forgive me, Custis. But a woman in my profession finds it difficult to stop acting. I'd almost forgotten what it could be like to hold nothing back, to really let it rip. Thank you, Custis. It was most delicious."

He smiled. "My pleasure."

She frowned then. "How's your wound?"

"When you get a chance I'd appreciate it if you would look at it. I think it busted open again."

"Oh, my God," she breathed, sitting up quickly. "I'm so sorry!"

"Don't be," he said, chuckling. "It's not that serious."

"I'll be right back," she told him, snatching up her robe and hurrying from the room.

An hour or so later, the sun planting long shadows on the nearly deserted street below, Longarm's wound freshly bandaged, he and Virginia had their breakfast at a table by the window, the two of them eating quietly, not needing much conversation.

After his second coffee, Longarm leaned back.

"I think I'll try again."

"Try what again?" Virginia asked, surprised, her face flushing.

He laughed. "That, too. But not right now. I mean get a hold of Pete Krueger."

"Didn't you get a chance to see him yesterday?"

"No. MacDonald and his drovers got to me first, the sheriff a willing accomplice."

"I don't trust that man, Custis."

"If you can believe it, I don't either."

Longarm got to his feet without further comment. Virginia went with him to the door. They kissed, almost chastely, and Longarm left her. The day before Virginia had told him how to get to Krueger's one-room shack, and as he pushed out through the saloon's batwings and glanced down Main Street, he was struck by the antic damage inflicted by the rampaging steers the night before and was pleased to see how little real damage had been done to the Golden Slipper's front. Only the lower step was gone, trampled into splinters, and a single porch post was knocked slightly askew.

Crossing the street, he did not try to avoid the unfriendly stares of those townsmen clearing up the debris in front of their shops. There was little doubt in Longarm's mind that they recognized him as the prisoner who had escaped their lynch party the night before. They were probably convinced as well that if he was not the author of the destruction they were now cleaning up, he sure as hell had something to do with it. Even so, not a single townsman planted himself in front of Longarm, or bothered even to hail him as he strode past. They had had their fill of him, evidently, and were probably ashamed of their behavior. Not only that, Longarm reflected grimly, the bottled courage they had drunk the night before they had long since pissed away.

As Longarm hurried across town, he found himself wondering where the Kid was holing up. If he was the one who had stampeded those cattle through town, he must be close by. Not that Longarm was worried much about the Kid. Obviously, as he had learned from the night before, he could take care of himself. In fact, there was a good likelihood that he was probably on his way to Virginia's apartment at that very moment.

When Longarm reached Krueger's place, he opened the gate in the white picket fence and started up the walk. There were chickens in back and they sounded a mite disturbed, even a little plaintive, as they scratched about. To his surprise, when Longarm mounted the low front porch, he found the front door slightly ajar.

Pushing it open cautiously, he stepped inside and closed the door softly behind him.

"Pete?" he called. "Pete Krueger."

There was no response. Longarm stiffened. He smelled trouble. The hair on the back of his neck lifted.

Then, from the bedroom came the Kid's voice. "Longarm?"

Startled, Longarm replied, "That you, Kid? It's me, all right."

"I'm in here, the bedroom."

Following the Kid's voice, Longarm left the small living room and entered the bedroom and saw the Kid sitting on the edge of the bed, staring bleakly at Longarm as he paused in the doorway. On the floor before the Kid, sprawled between the bed and the window, was a man's body. He was dressed only in his lower long

66

johns, and from the look of it, he had been shot in the chest. A gleaming pool of blood extended out from under his body.

Pete Krueger, Longarm guessed at once.

He hurried over and placed his fingers on the man's neck to see if he still had a pulse. But the cold chill of the man's flesh caused him to pull his hand back immediately. Stone dead, he was.

Standing up, he looked back at the Kid.

"He's dead, ain't he?"

"That he is, Kid."

"Jesus. Poor Pete."

"What the hell happened?"

"I wish I knew. I came in here this morning and someone whacked me on the head. Your steps on the porch just now woke me up.

Longarm looked down at the dead man. "He's been murdered."

"Yep. But see over there, by the door? It looks like Pete got in his own two cents."

Longarm walked over to the spot the Kid indicated and saw another, fresher bloodstain on the wood floor. He went down on one knee to examine it more closely. Part of the stain was as dry as the stain under Pete Krueger's body, but another portion was still gleaming wetly.

The Kid had left the bed and was standing beside him.

"I think I know what happened," he said bleakly. "Whoever did this thought Pete was unarmed when he drew on him. But Pete had a gun nearby, maybe under his pillow, and fired back, wounding the bastard who

67

shot him. He must've dropped him right here. He was out until I came in. That was when he ducked behind the door there"—he pointed at bloody footprints against the wall—"and waited for me to enter the room. When I did, he clubbed me and lit out."

"There should be more tracks outside then," Longarm said, stepping into the narrow hallway outside the bedroom.

And there were. Longarm followed the tracks into the kitchen and out the back door. From the length of the strides, it was clear the murderer was running when he left. There was only one footprint on the edge of the back porch as the man vaulted off it, his tracks vanishing once they reached the grass-covered backyard.

As Longarm returned to the kitchen, the Kid appeared in its doorway.

"Come see what old Pete left for us."

Longarm followed the Kid back into the bedroom. The Kid had already wrapped Pete's body in a bed sheet and deposited him on the bed. Striding past the bed to the spot where Pete had lain, he pointed to a section of the wooden floor close against the wall where Krueger had scrawled four letters with his own blood: D, E, C, K.

"Decker," said Longarm, his voice grim with anger. "He must have come in here sometime last night. During the stampede I'll bet. He caught Pete in bed and shot him."

"Why?" the Kid asked. "Why in hell would that son of a bitch want Pete dead?"

"I think I know why."

68

"Well, tell me then."

"I told Decker what I was doing here in Pawnee Wells. That I was after a bank robber wanted by the federal government. Pete Krueger knew who that man was and he was waiting for me to get here so he could finger him for me."

"Then the sheriff is the one you're after?"

"I don't think so. But Decker knows who he is, and he didn't want Pete to spoil things by telling me."

"You mean he's in with this bank robber?"

"That much is clear, I'd say."

The Kid's face hardened, his blue eyes burning with murderous intensity. "Then let's get him. Now."

"First things first. How's that bullet wound?"

"Sore as hell, but I'll live. It ain't me I'm thinkin' about now, it's what happened to Pete."

"We should get his body to an undertaker. Is there one in town?"

"Sure. But that'll cost."

"The government will pay. You might say Pete Krueger was on our payroll when he was killed. The thing is, I feel responsible."

"How come?"

"I never should have told the sheriff why I was in town, not until after I had spoken to Pete Krueger."

Longarm walked into the living room and slumped into a faded easy chair, a well-worn piece of furniture, one long since sculpted to the body of a smaller, frailer man.

"Kid, why don't you go find that undertaker," Longarm suggested to the Kid. "I'll wait here for you."

"All right. Just don't you try anything until I get back."

As soon as the Kid hurried out, Longarm got to his feet, watched from the window as the Kid vanished around a corner, then left the house.

If he was going to arrest the sheriff for the murder of Pete Krueger, he didn't think it would be smart to have the Kid along. He was too irate at this point, too eager to goad the sheriff into trying something foolish; Longarm didn't want that. He needed this sheriff alive.

If that was possible.

Chapter 5

The sheriff was not in his office. Frank Carson, however, was. He was seated at his corner desk, his entire right arm in a fresh cast that fairly gleamed as he rested it forward onto his desk top.

"You dirty son of a bitch," he said as Longarm strode into the office.

"You mean I'm supposed to let you slice me up?"

"Next time you won't see me comin'."

"There won't be a next time, Carson."

As Longarm spoke, he skirted the desk, reached down and grabbed Carson's collar. Hauling him out of his chair, Longarm flung him toward one of the cells. His cast dragging against the top of his desk, Carson stumbled back until he crashed into the cell door. Pulling himself in front of it, his eyes wild with fury, he rushed Longarm. Longarm ducked easily aside at the last moment, then punched the man solidly in his chops.

"I'm getting sick of this," Longarm muttered, doing his best to ignore the ripping pain in his side.

Carson rocked back, then made a clumsy attempt to swing his cast against Longarm's side. Longarm brushed it off almost casually and caught the man with a quick, powerful jab to the tip of Carson's jaw. Carson's eyes went glassy and his knees buckled. Longarm caught him before he hit the floor, pulled open the cell door, and flung him inside.

The keys were on top of Carson's desk. Longarm grabbed them and locked the cell door. Painfully, groggily, Carson hauled himself off the floor and onto the bunk.

"You bastard," he said thickly.

"Where's Decker?"

"Up yours."

"You don't know?"

"I know, you bastard, but what makes you think I'd tell you?"

Longarm unlocked the cell door and stepped into the cell. Advancing swiftly on the deputy, Longarm shoved his palm against the man's forehead so hard it slammed back against the wall. Then he poked the loaded key ring into Carson's mouth, the steel keys clashing harshly against the man's teeth.

"Tell me where Decker is," Longarm told Carson, "or you'll eat every damn one of them."

Carson tried to pull his head aside, but when at last he realized he could not free himself, he looked stubbornly away from Longarm, who pressed the keys deeper into the man's mouth. Carson began coughing as he tried once more to twist his head away. But Long-arm's pressure was inexorable.

Sweat pouring down his forehead, Carson finally gave in, nodding quickly, urgently. Stepping back, Longarm withdrew the keys from Carson's mouth. Coughing violently and spitting out blood, Carson leaned forward, holding his head with both hands. Watching him, Longarm thought Carson was going to get sick.

But he did not and told Longarm what he wanted to know. The sheriff was still in town and had been in earlier.

"How bad is he hurt?"

"It's a thigh wound. He's already gone to see the doc."

"Where is he now?"

"He said he was going back to his room."

"Which hotel?"

"The Nebraska House."

"What's his room number?"

"Find out for yourself, bastard."

Longarm slapped him.

"Jesus!" the man exploded, his eyes watering from the force of the blow. "What's the matter with you?"

"I'm impatient. What's Decker's room number?"

"Twenty-four."

Longarm stepped out of the cell and shut the door.

"Damn you," said Carson bitterly, "you'll regret this. And that's a promise."

"Holy shit, Carson, you got me trembling in my boots."

Longarm turned the key in the lock, chiding himself

mildly. Perhaps he shouldn't have been so rough on the deputy. But when he thought of Pete Krueger's sprawled body—a crime he had no doubt Frank Carson knew all about—he decided he wouldn't lose any sleep over it.

Dumping the keys on the desk top, Longarm left the jail and walked down a couple of blocks to the Nebraska House, aware with each step he took that his knife wound had opened again and would soon need attention. Entering the Nebraska House lobby, he mounted the narrow wooden stairs leading to the second floor and walked down the hallway to room number twenty-four and knocked.

"That you, Frank?" the sheriff called out warily.

Longarm cupped his hand up to his mouth. "Yeah, Ben, it's me."

"Shit! You don't sound like Frank."

Longarm stepped back and kicked the door; the heel of his boot struck beside the doorknob. The lock gave way as the panel splintered and the door swung wide, banging hard against the wall. Decker was sitting up on his bed, a gun in his hand. As Longarm ducked low and charged into the room, Decker flung up his gun and fired. The detonation filled the room with a deafening roar, the slug whining past Longarm's head; before Decker could fire a second time, Longarm's shoulder plowed into him, slamming him back onto the bed. With a howl of pain, Decker let his gun fall to the floor. Grabbing Decker by the neck, Longarm hauled him up to a sitting position, then stepped back, picked up the fallen gun and tossed it onto the dresser.

Decker's right thigh was heavily bandaged, Longarm noticed, his trouser leg stretched snugly over it.

"You ain't supposed to fire at law officers, Decker."

"You just broke into my room!"

"I had a reason."

"You're crazy, Long, comin' back here. You're wanted for the killing of them two Texas drovers, and for stampedin' them cattle last night."

"And I want you for the murder of Pete Krueger."

The sheriff's face went pale. "You must be crazy!"

"You deny it?"

"Of course I do. You're out of your head."

"The thing is, Decker, you didn't kill Krueger outright. He lived long enough to write your name on the floor. In his own blood. A pretty powerful bit of evidence, that. Even a Pawnee Wells jury will have no trouble convicting you on this one."

Drawn by the gunshot, footsteps pounded down the hall from the landing. Longarm turned to see a man he judged to be the hotel manager appear in the doorway. Behind him the desk clerk appeared, wide-eyed and panting. And from farther on down the hall came the excited murmur of the hotel's guests.

"I heard shots!" the manager cried. "And there's a bullet hole in the plaster across from the door."

"The sheriff fired at me," Longarm told him.

"He broke into my room, Keller," Decker told the man. "Throw him the hell out."

Ignoring the hotel manager, Longarm pulled Decker to his feet and steered the sheriff toward the door. He was just stepping into the hallway when MacDonald materialized in front of him. One look at Longarm with Decker and the trail boss reached back for his six-gun. Longarm flung the sheriff back into the room and reached for his .44—then froze as he found himself staring into the bore of MacDonald's Navy Colt.

"Don't do this, MacDonald," Longarm warned him. "You're making a big mistake here. I'm bringing Decker in. He's a murderer."

Decker, his six-gun in his hand, pushed past Longarm into the hallway. "Don't listen to this bastard, MacDonald. He's trying to push on to me what he just done."

"What's he done?"

"This son of a bitch killed a townsman. Pete Krueger."

As Decker spoke, he ducked swiftly past MacDonald to the second-floor landing and, limping grotesquely, continued on down the stairs

"Where you going, Decker?" MacDonald asked.

"I'll be right back, Mac," Decker called. "Just keep him there."

As Decker vanished down the stairs, Longarm turned to MacDonald.

"Put down that gun, MacDonald. You've just let a murderer escape."

"Decker? A killer? You must be crazy. *You're* the outlaw. Why in hell should I listen to you?"

"You should listen to me, MacDonald," Longarm said, his frustration mounting rapidly, "because I'm a lawman, a U.S. deputy marshal."

MacDonald laughed. "You expect me to believe that?"

"Would it help if I showed you my badge?"

"No, it wouldn't. You could've stole that badge from some lawman you bushwhacked." He waggled his

Navy Colt at Longarm. "Get on back into the room there, while we wait for the sheriff."

"You mean you actually expect Decker to return?"

"Never mind that. Just get on back into the room."

As Longarm did so, he heard the trail boss calling out to the manager, telling him and his clerk to go on downstairs, that he could handle this. As the two men hurried off down the hallway, MacDonald kicked the door shut behind him. Because Longarm had shattered its panel, it did not slam shut, he noticed.

"Put your hands over your head, mister," he said, walking toward Longarm, "and don't try nothing."

Longarm raised his hands. MacDonald stepped closer and took Longarm's .44, then lifted from his vest pockets the watch and derringer, tossing the lot roughly into a corner. Longarm winced as the pocket watch landed on its edge and rolled against the baseboard before flopping to the floor. As he sat wearily back onto the bed, the knife wound caused him to wince audibly.

"How long you going to keep me here, MacDonald?"

"Until the sheriff gets back."

"That's going to be a long wait. He's not coming back, I told you."

MacDonald glanced out the window uneasily. "He'll be back with his deputy. It won't be long. You'll see."

"What would it take to convince you I'm a U.S. deputy marshal?"

"More than your word. And more than flashing a badge at me."

"You know what, MacDonald?"

"What?"

"You're a big man and you brought all them cows up

77

here from Texas. That's the biggest trail herd I've seen in a long time. And I don't suppose it was an easy thing controlling a crew that size over such a long haul."

"You're right," MacDonald admitted warily, tossing his hat onto the top of the dresser. "I guess it wasn't so easy at that."

"And you know what else, MacDonald?"

"Well?"

"Even so, you're still the dumbest piece of shit that ever climbed onto a horse and rode north."

The man's weather-beaten face hardened. "Go ahead, Long. Rile me. You won't be all that sassy dancing on the end of a rope."

Brushing a long hand through his heavy thatch of white hair, MacDonald glanced quickly about the room, looking for a place to sit down. As he started over to a chair sitting by the window, the Pawnee Kid pushed the door all the way open and stepped silently into the room, his six-gun drawn. Doing his best to keep a poker face, Longarm watched as the Kid approached the big Texan from behind, lifted his gun high over his head and brought it down with ferocious force onto the Texan's head. With a barely audible sigh MacDonald toppled to the floor.

"What kept you?" Longarm asked the Kid as he went over to pick up his .44 and derringer.

"I didn't know where in hell you'd gone to, until I got a glimpse of the sheriff boiling out of the livery stable. The desk clerk was in the street downstairs by that time, telling anyone passing by what had just happened up here. He's likely informed half the town.

And right now the word's going around that you killed Pete."

"I figured that."

"You think maybe you can clear yourself with that bloody scrawl Pete left on the floor in his bedroom?"

"It does seem likely. But I'd say we've still got to bring Decker in."

"So what are we waiting for?"

Longarm shook his watch and held it up to his ear. Nothing. With a sigh he dropped it into his vest pocket, tucked the derringer into the other one, and led the way out of the hotel room.

When Decker pushed open the bedroom door, he saw at once the letters etched in blood on the floor by the bed. It was his name, all right—or most of it. That son of a bitch Long was right. This here piece of evidence would be enough to hang him, even in this town. He shook his head in wry admiration for that damned old coot. He not only put a slug in him, but he had managed to point the finger at him from beyond the grave.

Well, goddamn it, maybe he could do something about that finger.

He had passed a kerosene lamp sitting on the kitchen table. He went back for it, returned to the bedroom and hurled the lamp at the floor. As the kerosene exploded from the base, he thumbed a match to life and flung it at the shattered lamp. There was a small *whump* as the kerosene exploded. He stood there for a moment longer, watching the flames leap up the wall and begin devouring the curtains. As they roared across the ceiling, the sudden, furnace-like heat was enough to drive Decker from the room.

Slamming the door shut, he turned and rushed out the back door. Catching the reins of his waiting horse, he pulled himself painfully into his saddle and, keeping to the back alleys, headed across town to the jail. Dismounting in the alley behind it, he limped inside and saw Carson in one of the cells.

"What are you doing in there?" he demanded.

"Just get me the hell out, Ben."

"Don't know if I should."

"Do it, damn it. Get me out of here. Don't forget, I'm a witness. I know why you went over to see Pete last night, and I saw you when you came back."

"You know, I was just thinkin' the same thing."

Decker unlocked the cell door and pulled it open. Carson slipped quickly out past Decker, despite the awkwardness of his cast. As he took his holster and gun belt down from its peg beside his desk, Decker watched him thoughtfully.

"How'd that son of a bitch know where I was, Frank?"

"Aw, hell, Ben. The whole damn town knows you got a room at the Nebraska House."

"They don't all know my room number."

"So I told him. He was shoving the key ring down my gullet."

"A fat lot of help you are, Frank," Decker said meanly.

"What's the matter with you? He didn't get you, did he?"

"He would've if that knucklehead MacDonald hadn't

butted in. Right now, he's holding Long up in my room."

"So what do we do?"

"You mean you don't know?"

"Light out?"

"That's right. I'm headin' for Black Cliff. I got kin there."

"You mean you're runnin' from Long?"

"Of course I am. Don't you understand anything? We take care of him out in the open now and there'll be a dozen of them bastards comin' down on us. This here's Billy Vail and the federal government we're buckin'. I know Vail from way back. He's a tough nut. All I can hope now is that damn fool Texan takes care of that deputy long enough for me to light out."

"Go ahead then. Light out. Me, I'll just hang around. See what happens."

"You can't do that, Carson. Not now. Not after what I just told you."

In the difficult, clumsy act of buckling on his gun belt, Carson looked up at Decker. "What in the hell you mean by that, Ben?"

"Figure it out. You just now said it yourself. You know I killed Pete. Your testimony could hang me. And now you know where I'm headin'."

"So what's that supposed to mean?"

"It means you come with me or you stay here—and die."

"Hey, now look, Ben, there ain't no cause for you to talk to me like that."

"Then ride out with me. I can use another gun."

"How far do you think I can get with this damned cast on?"

"Take it off and wrap your elbow tight with a fresh bandage."

"You crazy? That son of a bitch Long broke my elbow. It's busted bad, Ben. I need this cast."

"Keep it on then. We'll ride out of here together just the same."

"No, Ben," the deputy said stubbornly. "I ain't goin' nowhere. You go ahead without me. You don't need to worry none. You got my word. You can trust me. I won't tell no one anything."

"Shit, Frank. My mother told me I couldn't trust nobody, and she ain't been proved wrong yet." Decker took out his six-gun and leveled it at Carson.

"Hey, wait a minute, Ben."

Decker cocked his revolver. "You comin' with me?"

"Ben! I can't *ride*!"

Decker aimed low and fired point-blank into Frank's gut. The bullet's impact drove the man back against his desk. Decker lifted the muzzle a notch and fired a second time, planting a neat hole in Frank's chest, just over his heart. An astonished look on his face, Frank slid to the floor, the cast slamming the floor loudly.

Decker grabbed two boxes of cartridges off the table, took down his Winchester from the wall rack, then hurried out the back door, still limping painfully. He heard townsmen in the street, obviously drawn by the two gunshots, yelling and running toward the jail. Then he heard, above the tramp of running feet, a more distant cry . . . Fire!

Decker grinned. These stupid-·bastards wouldn't know which way to turn now.

Dragging his injured thigh over the cantle, he turned his horse and set off down the alley. Approaching the feed mill at the end of town, he lifted his horse to a canter and was putting the town behind him when he heard a shout, then a familiar voice calling his name. Glancing back, he saw Bud Gunther, his eye patch seeming to obscure his entire face, running down Main Street after him.

Too late, you poor bastard, Decker muttered to himself. You an' Del will have to rob that goddamn bank without me.

Not slowing or even waving to Bud Gunther, Decker turned back around in his saddle, lifted his black to a gallop and kept on until he was well out onto the prairie; then he slowed to a trot. Occasionally he glanced back to look for sign of pursuit; for a maddeningly long while, it seemed, the buildings of Pawnee Wells remained visible on the horizon as they trembled in the heat radiating from the prairie's surface. When at last the town dropped from sight, Decker relaxed somewhat. Riding over the prairie, the grass closing behind him like ocean waves, he felt like a ship at sea, leaving no trace of his passage.

As he had told Frank Carson, he was heading for his kinfolks. They lived in and around the town of Black Cliff, deep in the South Dakota badlands. He had made this trip back often enough, most recently on the occasion of his youngest sister's marriage the summer before. It would take him a day of steady riding to reach the sand hills, he knew, and two days later he'd reach

Black Cliff, and once there, his kin would give him all the cover he would ever need.

He'd have no worries then about Long, or any other damn fool lawman they might send after him.

Decker felt himself begin to wilt under the sun's relentless glare. He stopped regularly to give the horse a taste of water from his canteen, and sometimes limped painfully alongside to save it. It would be all over for him if this black gave out on him. About three in the afternoon, he came in sight of a line of cottonwoods flanking a stream and knew he was on track. It took him two more hours of steady riding to reach the trees and when he got there, he was almost desperate to cool off in the stream, then make camp in the delicious coolness their shade would provide.

But first things first. For the past hour or so, his thigh wound had begun to throb with a near disabling intensity. He would have to tend to that first, maybe pour some fresh whiskey over it.

Just before riding into the trees, he took one glance back at the horizon.

"Shit," he said aloud.

Pulling up to peer more closely at the wavering shadows sitting above the shimmering horizon, he waited a full minute or two until the shadows materialized into two separate riders, disembodied, floating above the hazy heat. He turned back around in his saddle and rode on into the trees. He had time to get ready. But there were two of them, and he had a pretty good idea who they were.

Long and the Pawnee Kid.

Chapter 6

When Longarm and the Kid left the Nebraska House they were among the first to catch sight of the dark plume of smoke lifting into the sky from the other side of town. They fell in with the crowd running toward the fire and a few moments later found themselves standing in front of what remained of Pete Krueger's house.

The Kid swore. "My God, Longarm. Did you tell Decker what Pete left on that floor?"

Longarm nodded unhappily. "I did."

They joined the bucket brigade already formed, everyone working so hard that no one looked up long enough to recognize either the Kid or Longarm. By the time Longarm and the Kid got there, the fire had already broken through the roof so that the bucket brigade's efforts were directed primarily at wetting down adjacent structures. Pete's house was soon a smoking ruin, and when Longarm and the Kid picked their way over the charred beams and fragments of plaster to what remained of the bedroom, they found no trace at all of Pete's bloody message.

"Look there," said the Kid, pointing to the blackened remains of a kerosene lamp, its bowl shattered. Just beneath it was a nearly-burned-through floorboard. Decker had sure as hell burned his bridges behind him. Getting rid of this damning evidence in such a forthright fashion was a smart move, but it was a desperate one as well. Decker was a man in full flight now; this charred building was clear testimony to that fact.

"Let's move out, Longarm," the Kid said grimly. "We're wasting time here."

"Hold on, Kid. I want this bastard as much as you do. But we can't go riding off in all directions. I say we go check with Carson. Maybe he'll know which way the bird has flown."

When they got to the jail, they found another, smaller crowd milling in front of it; and as they pulled up behind it, they saw Frank Carson being carried out of the jail by three men, his bullet-riddled body resting full length on a wooden bench, his oversized cast resting on his chest. The undertaker, waiting for them at the foot of the jail's steps, turned and led the grim procession off to his parlor.

"Who did it?" the Kid asked a townsmen standing in front of him.

"Beats the shit out of me, Kid."

"Hell, I know who done it," a shrunken little man with bowed legs volunteered.

"Who?" the Kid asked him.

"Why, they ain't no question. That rustler Long—that big tall drink of water MacDonald's after, the one who stampeded them cattle through town last night. He's the one did it, I'm thinkin'."

Other members of the crowd moved closer then to join in the discussion. But as they did so, they were able to get a better look at the man standing by the Kid. They all knew the Kid well enough, and by this time, along with nearly everyone else in town, they were aware that the Kid had ridden into town with the same tall stranger who had broken out of jail the night before. And now they saw that same tall drink of water standing next to the Kid.

The townsmen halted, confused, as did the wiry little man who had just spoken with such bland assurance to the Kid. Like the rest, it was suddenly dawning on him that an unlucky fate had brought him face to face with the man he had just accused of killing Frank Carson.

His face lost its color.

"You know who I am, mister?" Longarm asked.

"Yeah, sure," the little townsman said nervously, edging back slightly.

"You still all that certain I shot down Frank Carson?"

"Hell, no. I ain't certain sure. I was just—"

"Maybe you shouldn't jump to conclusions, friend," Longarm told him, his voice almost gentle.

"You just got good advice, Tompkins," the Kid chimed in grimly. "This here's my good friend, Custis Long. He's a U.S. deputy marshal out of Denver, and he don't go around rustlin' cattle, no matter what that asshole MacDonald says."

"Sure, sure, Kid. I don't put no trust in MacDonald."

"That's smart, Tompkins. Real smart."

As Tompkins edged back into the crowd, the big fellow Longarm had tangled with the day before—the one with the black eye patch—came charging up the middle of the street, his heavy boots pounding.

"Hey, fellers," he cried to the dispersing crowd. "I just saw the sheriff!"

"Where is he, Gunther?" someone asked.

"He's ridin' out!"

"Did you tell him about Carson?"

"He wouldn't stop!" Gunther told them, pulling up. He was panting from his run and took a red bandanna from a back pocket and began mopping his face. As the crowd gathered close around him, he explained further: "I yelled to him, but he just kept on riding, like a bat out of hell."

Another townsman pushed through the crowd to pull up in front of Gunther. "Was Decker after someone?"

"Hell, no. He wasn't after no one. I told you. He just rode out. He saw me wavin' at him, but he wouldn't stop."

Noting the stunned faces of the townsmen, Longarm saw clearly how difficult it was for them to accept the implications of what Gunther had just told them. Difficult, but not impossible, for they all knew of Pete Krueger's murder. That the same man who had shot Pete had probably killed the deputy as well was almost a certainty. And now Gunther had seen the sheriff fleeing town, unwilling even to pull up in answer to Gunther's frantic waving.

The sheriff was responsible for both deaths.

Shocked, confused, the members of the crowd pulled back from Gunther, breaking into smaller groups and talking together in low, excited voices as they moved off. Longarm and the Kid overtook Gunther. When the glowering, heavyset tough recognized Longarm, his eye patch twitched a notch. His right wrist, Longarm noted, was clumsily bandaged, the end of one splint clearly visible. Mouth clenched angrily, scowling, Gunther held his ground.

"We want some information, Gunther," Longarm told the man.

"Blow it out your ass, Long."

"That ain't polite," the Kid told him. "And you sure as hell ain't in no condition to give us any shit."

"Where was Decker heading?" Longarm asked Gunther.

For a moment it appeared Gunther might not cooperate. Then, abruptly, he shrugged. "Decker was headin' north, the badlands."

"Why?"

"He's got kin up there."

"Where in particular."

"Place called Black Cliff."

"You sorry to see him go, are you, Bud?" asked the Kid.

"Stuff it, Kid."

Leaving Gunther, Longarm and the Kid moved off quickly down the street, heading for the Golden Slipper to pick up their gear. Without needing to discuss it, both men knew what lay ahead of them if they were to overtake Ben Decker: hard riding and a lot of luck.

• • •

Once they were well out on the prairie, Longarm was content to let the Kid take the lead. The Kid's tracking skills were phenomenal. With a keenness of discrimination Longarm could only envy, he spotted every bent blade of grass or broken stalk. Over and over he dismounted to uncover barely visible hoofprints hidden under grass clumps or on partially concealed sandy patches. And though they were riding across a featureless expanse unmarked by any apparent landmarks, the Kid rode across the prairie as unerringly as if he had an inbuilt compass. Even the lack of game had a special significance to the Kid, indicating that a rider—in this case Decker—had recently passed that way.

They caught sight of Decker not long before he reached a line of cottonwoods bordering a stream. Just before Decker reached the trees, he paused to look back. It was obvious he saw them.

"Damn," said the Kid, as Decker vanished into the trees. "He saw us. And he'll have plenty of cover in those cottonwoods."

"We better split up," Longarm suggested, "and flush him—come at him from both sides."

"And do it before it gets dark."

At once they lifted their horses to a gallop. Halfway to the line of trees they split up, Longarm cutting west, the Kid east.

Aware he had enough time to fill his canteens and quench his horse's thirst, Decker did just that. Then he tugged off his Levi's and lifted the bandage to take a look at his thigh wound. It looked as ugly as a whore's pucker and hurt a whole lot worse. He took out his whiskey flask, saturated the bloody bandage, poured a stiff dose into the wound, then tied the bandage back on. Grimacing from the pain, he pulled his Levi's over the thigh, the snug fit preventing the bandage from riding up. By this time the bandage was biting into the wound pretty deep, and he had some difficulty keeping himself from crying out.

Returning to the edge of the cottonwoods, he saw the two riders—close enough now for him to see each face clearly—split up as they approached the trees. At once Decker took heart. They were trying to flush him, hoping to drive him out into the open. Well now, he would just play the cards dealt him. And that meant he would have to move on each one separately.

He glanced up at the sky. He had less than a half hour of daylight left. It would have to do.

He went back to his horse, mounted up and splashed across the stream until he reached a clump of willows dense enough for his purpose. Dismounting, he grabbed the horse's bridle and yanked him down onto its side. Binding its front legs together with his hobbles to prevent the animal from regaining its feet, he left the horse and splashed back across the stream, on his way to meet the Kid.

He kept low and stayed close by the edge of the stream. When he caught sight of the Kid, the breed was riding cautiously through the shallow creek, keeping close by the bank, his head swinging alertly from side to side as he peered into the trees and brush on either side. Placing his hat down on the bank, Decker slipped into a patch of reeds, the water's sudden chill welcome as it soaked through his Levi's to cool his thigh wound. Cautiously, so as to cause no ripples, he moved away from the bank out into the reeds until the water was as high as his waist. He heard the Kid's horse splashing closer and took out his knife and squatted down into the reeds until the icy water lapped his chin.

Horse and rider came nearer, the horse snorting and shaking its head, perhaps in protest at having to slog through the streambed's clinging mud. Decker kept himself perfectly still, the knife in his hand out of sight under the water. The Kid, his eyes on the bank, passed between it and Decker, looming so close that the combined bulk of horse and rider momentarily shut out the night sky. Gritting his teeth against the pain he knew he would feel when he made his move, Decker heaved upward out of the water, slashing out at the Kid's thigh. He missed, then grabbed the Kid's foot with his left hand and yanked hard, trying to drag the Kid off his horse. Lashing out with his foot, the Kid kicked Decker backward. In the deep, clinging water Decker lost his balance for a moment. The Kid swung his horse so that it was facing him head on, then reached back for his side arm. Decker saw the dull gleam of its barrel, and ducking closer, grabbed the horse's bridle. Pulling the animal's head closer to him, he slashed up brutally, his blade slicing deep into the brute's neck.

A powerful, drenching gout of blood exploded from the horse's neck. It went down heavily, its bulk smacking against the water like a gunshot. Caught under the horse, the Kid thrashed wildly in an effort to free himself. But the shallow water and the weight of the horse combined to keep him trapped, and before he could scramble free, Decker fell on him, repeatedly sinking his knife into the struggling man's body.

"Breed!" he cried with each slash. "Dirty breed!"

Drawing back only when he heard the pound of approaching hoofs, Decker sheathed his knife and dove into the water; keeping low, at times ducking completely under the shallow water, he made it across the stream. Gaining the cottonwoods on the other side, he ran downstream to his horse.

As soon as he untied the hobbles, the horse sprang upright, shaking its head angrily, blowing all the while. Decker snatched the reins, pulled the horse around and hauled his drenched body into the saddle, his thigh wound throbbing now. Breaking from the cottonwoods on the other side of the stream, he headed north again over the prairie. Dusk was falling rapidly. He hadn't gone long before he heard a horse splashing across the stream behind him; that would be the other one—Long.

He bent forward over the black, his heels digging hard into its steaming flanks. Behind him, Long broke out of the cottonwoods and sent a shot after him. But at that distance and with night falling, Decker paid little attention, and without bothering to look back, he swept on across the grassland. He could hear Long gaining on him, but he had confidence in his black's superior stamina and just kept going. Long did not fire again, and when Decker was a few miles farther on, he glanced back and saw that Long was falling steadily behind.

Darkness fell with a suddenness that was startling, and he lifted his horse to one last great spurt, keeping on until he felt the horse finally begin to give out. Urging it on until he dropped into a swale, he halted abruptly and swung from his saddle, pulling the animal down beside him. The grass here was high enough to conceal him and the horse. Lying prone close beside the horse's head, he clamped his left hand over the horse's dripping muzzle to keep it quiet, then lifted his head slightly to watch as Long, bent low over his mount, loomed closer.

Decker cocked his revolver, tracked the oncoming rider, and waited patiently. But Long never got closer than thirty yards as he charged on past him into the night. Decker waited. Long's hoofbeats faded, then died out completely. And still Decker waited. At last there came the distant pound of hooves as Long returned. It was a great deal darker by now and though this time Long swept past Decker much closer than before, he did not slow down. In a moment the night had swallowed him. When the pound of hoofbeats faded completely, Decker pulled his horse upright, mounted up, and rode on, this time content to keep his horse at a steady, un-hurried trot.

When the sun's red eye broke above the plains to his right, he stopped for about a half hour to rest himself and the black, then set out again, alternately walking and riding. He reached a pothole lake around noon and took a short nap, then moved out again, allowing him-self only the briefest of stops whenever a stream or sinkhole allowed. He maintained this pace through the day and on through the night. Toward the end of the following day a sudden storm overtook him, lashing him and the horse with stinging tendrils of rain, the wind gusts at times nearly blowing him out of the saddle.

But this Decker did not mind. Despite the deafening thunderclaps and the searing forks of lightning that played about him, he counted the rain as a blessing, since he had not come upon any water since that morning. Head bent into the wind, he rode on steadily, allowing his body to drink in the water retained by his drenched clothes. On the next day, riding under a brilliant, cloudless sky, the sun pressing on his back like a branding iron, he watched the skies hopefully, this time praying for another storm.

Late that night he reached the badlands and kept on until he saw ahead of him a familiar pillar of rock looming against the night sky.

Reining in, he cocked one ear, and before long he caught the sound of water splashing on rock. Following the sound, he soon reached a familiar spring-fed pool. He slid wearily off his mount onto the patch of sand bordering the pool and tethered the horse to a sapling. Hobbling painfully to the edge of the pool, he filled his hat with water and brought it back to the black, careful not to let the horse gulp down too much at a time. Only when the horse's thirst had been quenched did he allow himself to drink his fill.

Off-saddling the black then, he filled his canteen. Only then did he sit down on a rock shelf to examine his thigh. The pain of it had been his only companion since leaving the cottonwoods, and the wound continued to swell under his pants leg like an obscene egg. When he peeled off his Levi's and unrolled the heavy, scabbed-over bandage, he could see even in the dim light of the stars that the wound needed to be opened up again.

He took out his knife and without pause raked the blade across the swollen scab. The blood broke through, carrying with it in a long, yellowish stream the festering poison that had been accumulating. Unscrewing his flask, Decker poured the whiskey into it. This time the pain was such that he could not hold back. For a long, eerie moment his howling cry echoed throughout the badlands, seeming at the last of it to stun the night into an unnatural, waiting stillness.

A few moments later, sweat pouring down his face, Decker pulled his Levi's back on without bothering to rebandage the wound. Tipping the flask up, he drained its contents, and then, leaning back against the rock shelf, he shattered the night once again—this time with laughter, triumphant laughter.

Goddamn it to hell! He had made it!

He might be missing a leg before this week was out, but he had cut that damned half-breed into buffalo jerky and before another day had passed, he would be deep inside the badlands, safe with his own kin.

And if and when that U.S. deputy marshal came up here after him, he'd never see Denver or that fool Vail again.

Chapter 7

When Longarm returned to the spot by the stream where he had left the Kid, the Kid asked, "Did you get him?"

"No," Longarm replied, dismounting.

"What are you doing here then? Leave me be and go after him. You know where he's headin'."

"Sure I know he's heading. But I'm not leaving you here like this."

"Why not? It's as good a place as any."

Without bothering to answer, Longarm peeled off the Kid's bloody shirt. The wounds were almost too numerous to count. Fortunately, most of them were superficial with only two that looked serious, one under the left shoulder blade, the other in his side, close by the old bullet wound. He was losing blood steadily and Longarm tore a blanket into strips and bound the wounds tightly enough to reduce some of the bleeding.

Anxious to get the Kid to a doctor, Longarm set out for Pawnee Wells at once, the Kid riding up behind him, his arms locked around Longarm's waist. Longarm did not push the horse, but by morning, he felt it trembling unsteadily under him and the two dismounted.

Longarm gave the Kid his fill from the canteen, took two large swallows himself, then poured water into the palm of his hand and wet the horse's nostrils, then let it lick the rest of the water from his hand. Only gradually did he give the horse enough to finally quench its thirst, after which he fed it some grain, helped the Kid back up into the saddle and led the horse on foot from there.

But the horse had already given most of what it had to give the night before; a few miles farther on it staggered once, sighed heavily, and plunged to its knees. The Kid managed to jump free before it collapsed on its side, lather bubbling from its lips, too far gone even to raise its head.

"We'll have to shoot it," the Kid told Longarm.

"No."

Longarm forced some water into the horse's mouth and tied the grain bonnet about its neck. Then he stripped the saddle off it, wrapped the bedroll around his rifle, and buried the saddle in a shallow sand pit a few feet away near a prairie dog mound.

"You'll forget where you left it," the Kid said.

"No, I won't. Look."

He pointed to a line of three prairie dog towns pointing straight at this one mound.

"I still think you won't find it."

"I'll find it."

They both looked back at the horse then.

"It might make it yet," Longarm said, "once the sun goes down and it's had a chance to rest."

"Maybe," the Kid said, but he didn't sound optimistic.

They turned their backs on the horse and trudged on. The Kid had trouble keeping up, and Longarm was forced to slow to his pace. They could not be that far from Pawnee Wells, Longarm reasoned, but though they kept on until nightfall, no welcome mirage appeared to beckon them on. By then, Longarm was all but holding up the Kid as he stumbled along beside him. When at last they stopped to make camp for the night, the Kid collapsed to the ground, feverish and barely coherent.

Longarm looked over the Kid's wounds and wished he hadn't. He bandaged them up again to the best of his ability, after which he dined on biscuits and beef jerky, washing it down with coffee.

The Kid was too miserable to eat much.

"I'm on fire, Longarm," he told him. "I just don't feel hungry."

"You should eat something. It'll keep up your strength."

"No, it won't. It'll make me throw up."

"Have it your way."

Longarm stomped out the fire.

"I been thinkin'," the Kid said.

"That so?"

"I want you to leave me here. I want you to go on without me."

"That ain't very clear thinking."

"For Christ's sake, listen to me, Longarm! There's no way I can make it through another day like this. And

99

I'll only be holding you back. Just leave me here."

Longarm draped his slicker over the Kid and climbed into his bedroll. It took him awhile to get comfortable without his saddle to use as a pillow, but he used his cross-draw rig instead, worked his hip into the soft ground and closed his eyes.

"We'll get an early start tomorrow," he told the Kid.

The Kid did not reply.

Assuming the matter was closed, Longarm fell almost immediately asleep. How long he slept, he had no idea, but when he awoke it was suddenly and with a start.

Something was wrong.

Pushing himself up onto his elbows, he glanced over at the Kid. The slicker remained, but the Kid was gone. Longarm jumped to his feet. The half moon lent a faint, pale sheen to the grasslands surrounding him, but he could not see the Kid.

"Kid!" he cried. "Hey, Kid!"

There was no response, not that Longarm had expected any.

He turned about him then, studying the ground, and after a short while found what appeared to be the Kid's trail. Unable to walk, he had left the campsite by dragging himself through the grass. But the grass was damp with dew by this time, and his body left a clear path as it bent under his passage. For someone who had decided he was too weak to go on, the Kid managed to cover a considerable distance before Longarm found him close to dawn, lying facedown at the bottom of an old buffalo wallow. Longarm turned him over. The Kid's face was flushed and his breathing was fitful. Picking him up in his arms, Longarm returned to the camp with him and slapped him awake, then gave him some water.

The Kid choked some on the water, then gulped it down. "How'd I get back here?"

"I carried you."

"How'd you find me?"

"Just followed your track."

"How could you?"

"The grass you dragged yourself through was wet."

The Kid nodded wearily, understanding at once. "You were snoring when I crawled off. I figured you'd sleep till daylight. The grass would have dried off by then and sprung up again. What made you wake up?"

"Never mind. The important thing is I did. That was a damn fool stunt you pulled and I resent it."

"Why?"

"I got a long day ahead of me and I could've used the sleep."

"Damnit, I already told you. There's no way I can go with you."

"Look, Kid, you think I can find my way back to Pawnee Wells across this emptiness without your help? Hell, that sun has fried my brains already. I might end up going in circles."

"All right," the Kid said wearily. "Give me some of that hardtack. Maybe I can keep it down."

The Kid chewed doggedly on what remained of the hardtack, and when he was done, Longarm handed him the water canteen. Then they set off. By noon, despite the hardtack he had consumed, the Kid was far gone, unable to take another step, and no longer alert enough to keep them on course.

The Kid sagged to the ground. He was on fire. Longarm soaked his bandanna with some of the little water that remained in his canteen and dabbed at the Kid's face. The cooling compress brought him around for a while, but almost immediately he lost consciousness again, and Longarm gave up the effort when he realized how little water they had left.

He sat back wearily on his elbows and rested his bones, staring in the direction they were heading, searching for some sign of Pawnee Wells. A single horseman or head of cattle would have been enough to give him the strength and sense of progress he needed to keep going. Even a herd of pronghorn on the skyline would have been appreciated. But within his line of sight in all four directions, nothing moved under the clear, glaring sky.

He took one more sip of the water, then got wearily to his feet.

"You ready, Kid?"

The Kid's lips barely moved. "Leave me here."

Longarm bent, grabbed the Kid by the waist, and flung him over his shoulder. He hefted him for a moment to get comfortable, then moved out. He knew that only an about face in his luck would bring him and the Kid to Pawnee Wells before he gave out, but he thrust that grim awareness from his mind as he moved doggedly ahead, eyes on the ground before him, concentrating now on simply placing one foot ahead of the other.

His progress was maddeningly slow as the sky wheeled drunkenly about him, at times almost succeeding in destroying his sense of direction. Sweat poured off him in a continual stream, drenehing his upper body, adding still more to the weight he had to carry. Whenever he stopped to rest, it resembled more a collapse than anything else; and with each stop he took, he found it more agonizingly difficult to heave himself upright and continue on. On he plodded, unable to gauge any progress as he struggled over the surface of this vast, treeless expanse of grassland. Time lost all significance, and whenever he glanced up at the sky to locate the sun, its placement in the firmament only confused him further.

He was reeling like a drunken sailor when he stumbled without warning upon the torn-up ground broken by the trail herds heading for Pawnee Wells. For a second or two, so exhausted was he, its significance was lost on him and he was well onto the beaten trail before he pulled up, blinking, and realized what he had found. He would have laughed out loud if his mouth were not so dry. Shifting the Kid to his other shoulder, he changed direction and followed the chewed-up trace, this time at a brisker pace, renewed by a fresh surge of hope. How long he kept on the trace, he had no idea. Twice the uneven, chewed-up ground caused him to stumble and fall to his knees. But each time he swore, straightened up under his burden and plodded on.

The sun, a huge red eye, was resting on the western horizon when Longarm glanced up and saw ahead of him the water tower and frame buildings of Pawnee Wells. It was as if they had just popped up on a dark serving tray. He tried to increase his pace, but only succeeded in stumbling over a loose clod of dirt. He went down, the Kid's heavy body thumping to the ground beyond him.

Sitting up, Longarm peered with bitter exasperation at the distant buildings. He could not believe he had come this far only to fail. He looked down at the Kid.

"I'm going on alone, Kid," he told him. "I'll be back for you. That's a promise."

He might as well have been talking to himself. The Kid was completely out of it.

Longarm heaved himself upright and plodded on toward Pawnee Wells. The fact that he no longer had to cope with the Kid's weight enabled him to go a good distance before he caught sight of a rider south of him heading toward the town. Longarm took off his hat and waved it. The rider saw him, took off his own hat and waved back, turning his horse toward him at the same time.

When he reached Longarm, he reined in his horse, and peered down at him. "What in the hell are you doing out here afoot, mister?"

"That's a long story."

"You don't look so hot." The rider nudged his horse closer and reached his hand down to Longarm. "Swing up behind me and I'll take you into town."

"No. We've got to go back. The Kid's out there."

"The Kid?"

"That's right."

"You talkin' about the Pawnee Kid?"

Longarm nodded wearily.

"You can walk, then. He's a damned breed and a cattle rustler."

Longarm drew his six-gun and aimed up at the rider.

104

"Dismount, friend, and move away from your horse."

"I might a knowed," he said. "Any friend of the Kid."

Compressing his lips angrily, the rider dismounted. Still covering the man, Longarm hauled himself onto the horse, turned it, and headed back to where he had left the Kid. Dismounting, he lifted him up onto the horse. Momentarily conscious, the Kid mumbled something in protest at Longarm's rough handling. Ignoring it, Longarm mounted up behind him and headed on a trot for Pawnee Wells. As he skirted the man he had left afoot, he called out to him, promising to leave his mount in the town livery.

When Longarm reached Pawnee Wells' Main Street, he noticed how empty the town seemed and wondered if this could mean that MacDonald and his trail herd had pulled out for Omaha. Now that he thought of it, he had seen no trace of the trail herd north of the town. If Mac-Donald had pulled out, this would simplify matters mightily. Dismounting in front of the Golden Slipper, he ignored the rapidly growing crowd and, hefting the Kid onto his shoulder, mounted the porch and pushed through the batwings into the saloon.

He took only a few steps before a cry came from the back of the room.

"Custis!"

He halted as Virginia rushed up to him.

"The Kid's hurt," he told her. "Give me a hand, will you?"

"My God! What happened?"

"Ben Decker. He cut the Kid up pretty bad."

Virginia called over a barkeep and one of her

bouncers. On her orders, they lifted the Kid off Longarm's shoulders and carried him toward the stairs leading to her apartment. Waving over one of the gamblers, Virginia told him to get the doc. The gambler left the saloon on the run.

Virginia looked at Longarm, concern etched on her face. "You look like you just walked through hell, Custis. You going to be all right?"

He nodded wearily. "What about MacDonald?"

"On his way to Omaha. He's taken what's left of his herd and ridden out—with a very sore head, I might add. Early this morning we planted Pete and Frank Carson."

"I'm all right. Go look after the Kid."

With a quick nod, she hurried off. For a shaky moment Longarm watched her follow up the stairs after the Kid; then he moved over to the bar and asked for a bottle of Maryland rye and a glass. A moment later, sagging into a chair in the back, he poured himself a drink, dumped it down his parched throat, then started to pour himself another.

Before he could do so, he sagged forward onto the table and plunged headlong into an exhausted sleep.

Chapter 8

Virginia was standing beside Longarm's chair, shaking him awake. He raised his head and blinked away the tendrils of sleep still clinging to him. Virginia sat down beside him.

She nodded her head in the direction of the bar. "You got a visitor."

Longarm looked past her. The rider he'd left afoot outside of town was leaning back against the bar, his elbows resting on it. He did not look at all friendly. As soon as Longarm's glance met his, he spoke out loudly so everyone in the saloon could hear him.

"There he is, the son of a bitch who stole my hoss!"

His bold accusation quieted the saloon and froze every patron as they watched him put down his beer stein and walk the length of the saloon to Longarm's table.

When he reached it, he held up, rocking back on his heels. "I'm waitin' on you, mister."

"Waitin' on me? Why, man, you don't need to go and do that."

"I mean I'm callin' you out, mister!"

"Oh. You mean you want a gunfight outside in the street."

The man nodded stiffly. "I'm ready when you are."

Longarm shook his head wearily and glanced over at Virginia. "This is the second time I've been braced in here, Virginia. This is the *unfriendliest* saloon!"

Virginia laughed.

Longarm looked back at the man. "Your horse is right outside. Thanks for the loan of it. Now, for Christ's sake, forget all this Ned Buntline bullshit and join me in a drink."

The man stood there, irresolute, as if he had forgotten the rest of his lines and was waiting for someone to prompt him. He looked about the saloon in some confusion. A few amused faces met his glance. He looked down at Virginia. She was smiling openly at him.

"Sit down, Chet," she urged, "before I bust out laughing."

"Damnit, Virginia, this man's a hoss thief!"

"You heard the lady," Longarm told him. "Sit down and give me a chance to thank you for the loan of your horse."

The air went out of Chet's balloon. He shucked his hat back off his forehead and sat down. Longarm took a better look at him than he had out on the prairie. Chet was a man in his late twenties, slim waisted with shoulders wide enough to make him have to ease his way through a doorway. His thick thatch of brown hair was flattened down by his hat, his clear, dark eyes cheerful, despite the fact that at the moment he was trying very hard to keep the scowl on his long, lean face.

"Custis," Virginia said, "meet Chet Winston. He runs a horse ranch south of here."

As Longarm shook Chet's hand, Virginia introduced Chet to Longarm, explaining that he was a U.S. deputy marshal who had come all the way from Denver.

"A lawman?" Chet said, pushing back from the table slightly, as if to get a better look at Longarm. "Well, now. Fancy that."

Longarm looked at Virginia. "How about another glass."

Virginia waved over one of her girls and had her bring two glasses, one for Chet and one for herself. When the girl returned with the glasses, Longarm filled all three and they drank up.

Chet leaned back in his chair. "Don't mind if I admit it, this is good whiskey."

"This isn't whiskey. It's Maryland rye."

"My apologies."

"Accepted." Longarm turned to Virginia. "How's the Kid?"

"The doc's sewing him up now. He yelled a blue streak when I cleaned out his knife wounds, but the doc quieted him down with a shot of morphine."

"How bad's he been cut?"

"The doc said not to worry. He won't be able to pull on his boots for a while yet, but he'll live."

Longarm turned back to Chet. "How long you going to be in town?"

Chet shrugged.

"This town needs a deputy sheriff. Come with me and I'll swear you in."

"Me? Sheriff?"

"Why not?"

"Hey, now wait just a minute."

"You won't be deputy sheriff for long. Soon as I contact my chief in Denver, he'll get someone to come out here from Lincoln. Until then this town needs somebody."

"What about you?"

"I'm too damn tired."

"Yeah. You look tired. Hell, you look worse than tired."

Watching him closely, Longarm could see how the thought of wearing a star, if only for a short while, began to puff Chet up; though he would of course be the last to admit it. As Longarm well knew, there weren't too many men in their prime who would turn down the chance to wear a tin star.

"You sure you got the authority to appoint me deputy sheriff?"

"I'm sure."

"All right," Chet said, "I'll give it a shot—but not for long. I got a ranch to look after."

"A week at the most," Longarm assured him.

A moment later Longarm and the new sheriff left the saloon together.

110

• • •

Late the next morning, standing in the window of Virginia's bedroom, Longarm opened the telegram one of the barkeeps had just brought up to him.

STATE ATTORNEY GENERAL ON WAY FROM CAPITOL STOP YOU HAVE FULL AUTHORITY TO APPOINT NEW SHERIFF STOP NEVER TRUSTED BEN DECKER STOP FORGET HIM STOP FIND DELSEY STOP VAIL

Longarm showed the telegram to Virginia. She read it quickly and handed it back to him.

"Why the frown, Custis?"

"Vail has a one-track mind. Doesn't want me to go after Decker."

"This attorney general, how long will it take for him to get here?"

"Depends on when he leaves Lincoln."

"A couple of days, maybe?"

"I'd say that. Yes."

She stepped closer to him. "That's plenty of time."

"For what?"

"Don't you know?" She flung her arms around his neck.

"Guess I do at that," he said, kissing her on the lips.

"How's that knife wound?"

"Much better."

"Then I won't have to be so careful this time."

"Jesus. You mean you were holding back before?"

"I'll let you be the judge."

Longarm shucked off his robe, swept Virginia up in

111

his arms, carried her over to the bed, and dumped her onto it. Wriggling out of her gown, she lifted her arms to him. He dropped onto her. She opened her mouth. His lips closed about hers, his tongue probing deeply, hungrily. When he drew back, she lifted her head and fastened her teeth gently but firmly about his lower lip and pulled him back down, spreading her legs at the same time.

She was ready for him. More than ready. He could feel the hot moist warmth of her muff thrusting eagerly up against him. Her strong, practiced fingers closed about his erection and guided him into her with an almost angry urgency. He plunged on into her, probing so deep he could feel the tip of his erection strike bottom.

She laughed huskily and thrust her ample thighs still higher, then wrapped both legs around his waist, scissoring him. He felt the muscles of her vagina grabbing, then holding him as he continued thrusting wildly. The battering, mindless rhythm of it took hold and soon they were whaling away at each other like two crazy kids behind a barn. She began flinging her head from side to side, her eyes shut tightly, and a steady stream of invective came from her, the savage intensity of it sending a delicious tide of lust shivering up his spine.

He drove down into her, impaling her with a ferocity that matched her own. He felt her shudder under him as she let out a prolonged cry—more a wail of helplessness than of pleasure. It sent answering spasms through him and he began to come repeatedly; she came then also, crying out suddenly with almost frightening abandon. He clung to her fiercely, their mutual climaxes convulsing them both as they grew into each other, became one flesh, one single, twisting, moaning entity. . . .

Afterward, they ate a hearty breakfast. A very hearty breakfast, even though by that time Longarm was wondering if he didn't need to go back to bed and rest up some.

"With Pete Krueger dead, how are you going to find out who this Delsey fellow is?" Virginia asked, pouring fresh coffee into his cup.

"He's in town, somewhere, if he hasn't already flown."

"Do you think he has?"

"There's a chance of it."

"Why?"

"I figure Decker was working with him. With Decker gone, he's been left high and dry. Did you notice any townsman clearing out after that fire?"

"Not that I heard of."

"If anyone had, packing his belongings and leaving in the middle of the week, he'd attract plenty of attention."

"Yes, he would."

"Who *has* left town? Since the fire, I mean."

"One of my girls. She left yesterday on the evening stage, heading home to a sick mother. At the same time a whiskey drummer got off and another one got on, or rather was poured on. That's all the arrivals and departures since the fire, Longarm."

"Then Delsey is still in town."

"He could have rented a horse from the livery and ridden out."

"On my way back from the barbershop, I stopped in at the stable and checked out that possibility. No one's ridden out, and if anyone does, the hostler's going to get in touch with me, promptly."

She sighed. "Well, if he's still in town then, you better go find him."

"How many banks in town?"

"Only one. The Pawnee Wells National Bank."

"That's the only one?"

She nodded, sipping her coffee.

"In that case, it must be doing pretty well."

"It's full up, Custis. The ranchers and farmers hereabouts rely on it heavily. And there isn't a citizen in this town—and that includes me—without most of their savings in it. Cyrus Morgan is the president and he's a shrewd old bird who gives excellent interest to his depositers while charging top rates for the use of his money."

"I think I'd like to go meet this Cyrus Morgan. How about coming with me? You can introduce me to him yourself."

She put down her coffee quickly, blushing.

"Why, Custis. What on earth are you thinking of? I'm a lady of the night. I own and run a common saloon. Creatures of our stripe are not supposed to show themselves, at least not in broad daylight."

"There's nothing I'd like better than to shock the craven citizens of this town. So far, they haven't impressed me much at all."

"Nor me, either, Custis."

Reaching out, he took her hand in his. "You just put on your best bib and tucker, Virginia. We'll go out steppin'. The first citizen who fails to doff his hat or show you proper respect will find himself drinking from a horse trough."

"What a lovely thought." She got to her feet and headed for the bedroom.

"I'll be in Annie's room, checking on the Kid," he told her, getting up from the table and heading for the door.

Leaving Virginia's apartment, he walked down the hallway to a small room in the back and knocked softly on the door.

"That you, Longarm?" the Kid called.

"Yup."

"Come on in."

Longarm entered.

The Kid, his naked upper torso swathed in bandages, was sitting up in bed, an attentive, bright-eyed young girl sitting on the edge of it next to him. There was a steaming bowl of soup in her hand from which she was spoon-feeding him. At Longarm's entrance, she stood up quickly, nervously.

"Hi, Annie," Longarm said. "How's our patient doing?"

She glanced over at the Kid and blushed, and Longarm knew then that the Kid was coming along just fine.

"I was feedin' him some hot broth the cook made for him."

"All the comforts of home, Longarm," the Kid replied cheerfully.

"I got a reply from Vail. All he wants is for me to find John Delsey."

"Well, you go find him then. Leave Decker for me."

"You stay put, Kid. Right now you look like death warmed over. You lost a lot of blood, don't forget."

"I'm gettin' my strength back—fast." He grinned over at Annie. "Ain't that the truth, Annie?"

Again the girl blushed. Longarm was amused to see such an experienced lady of the night blushing over a tumble in the sack.

"Annie," Longarm said, "could you maybe go outside for a minute. I want to talk to the Kid."

"Oh, sure," she said.

She put the bowl of soup down on the night table and left the room.

Watching her scoot out the door, the Kid grinned. "A real fine lady, that. With her hair down, she's as wild as I am—almost."

Longarm pulled up a chair and sat down.

"You got any idea why Decker killed Pete Krueger?"

"Decker didn't want you to talk to Pete."

"Which means he was protecting John Delsey."

"That too."

"But why?"

"Beats the shit out of me, Longarm."

"Because he was planning to rob the local bank. And the sheriff was a part of it."

"Why would Delsey let him in on it?"

"To provide protection for Delsey and anyone else with him. I'd say they were planning to hit the bank as soon as MacDonald and his crew left town."

"So go find Delsey, then."

"That's why I'm off to see the bank president."

"You think *he* knows who Delsey is?"

"He might know more than he thinks he does."

"I don't get it, Longarm."

"If you were a bank robber and you came into town looking for work, where would you go?"

The Kid grinned. "To where the money is."

"The Pawnee Wells National Bank."

"You're right. What better way to case a bank?"

"My thinking exactly."

The Kid leaned back against his pillow. "On your way out, send Annie back in."

Virginia need not have worried about Cyrus Morgan's welcome. The bank president's greeting was hearty, generous, and a marvel of courtesy as he hurried to provide a more comfortable chair for her. The fact that Virginia was probably one of his largest depositors might possibly have had something to do with it, Longarm realized; but he did not believe that was all of it, and could sense the genuine respect and affection the old codger held for Virginia.

Morgan was a small spry barrel of a man in his late fifties with reddish hair and gray mutton-chop whiskers. The eyes that peered at them from behind his spectacles were as bright and as keen as silver dollars; it was clear that his prosperity and that of his bank were the elixir that kept his lifeblood coursing through his old veins.

As soon as Virginia was comfortable, Morgan offered Longarm a cigar, lighted it for him, then leaned back in his chair and regarded Virginia with genuine warmth.

"Well now, Virginia, to what do I owe this unexpected pleasure?"

"Cyrus, Mr. Long here needs your help."

Morgan's keen eyes shifted to Longarm. "And how can I help you, Mr. Long?"

"I'm looking for someone."

"And you think I can help you?"

"His name's John Delsey, but I'm sure he's using an alias."

"I know of no John Delsey in Pawnee Wells, Mr. Long. So perhaps you are right. And what is this Mr. Delsey's occupation?"

"He robs banks."

Startled, Morgan leaned forward, peering quizzically at Longarm, looking for some sign that Longarm was jesting. "Mr. Long, you are *not* joking, I see."

"The thing is, this Delsey might be working for you right now."

"Working for me?"

"As a teller, perhaps, or in some other capacity. Have you hired any newcomers to town recently?"

"Why, yes, I have. Two men. One is my janitor, the other a teller."

"Who else works here?"

"The chief cashier, Frank Wells. Mr. Wells has been with me for over ten years. I trust him implicitly."

Longarm turned in his chair and looked over at the bank counter.

"Which one is the new teller you hired?"

"At the last window, the gentleman in the green eyeshade."

Longarm peered at him closely. He wore thin, steel-rimmed spectacles, was as bald as a doorknob, and had black, bushy eyebrows. He did not match John Delsey's description.

"What about this janitor? Could you describe him to me?"

"There's not all that much to describe. He's a little over forty, I'd say, has sandy hair, brown eyes, I think. Not a big man, slight of build."

"How tall would you say?"

"Average."

"About five ten?"

"Yes."

"Does he have a mustache?"

"No, Del's clean shaven."

Longarm leaned forward. "What'd you say his name was?"

"Del. Del Johnson."

Longarm glanced at Virginia, then back at the little bank president. A man on the run is seldom able to make up a name that differs very much from his own. There is always a similarity, it seems. John Delsey and Del Johnson had that unmistakable resemblance. The fact that Del Johnson was clean shaven was not significant. It was no trick at all for a man to shave off his mustache.

"Could you bring this Del Johnson out? I'd like to meet him."

"I'm afraid that's impossible. He didn't show up for work today. His landlady stopped by earlier this morning and said he was not well."

"Do you have his address?"

"He lives in the Fordham rooming house."

Longarm glanced at Virginia. "Where's that?"

"I'll take you there."

"All right."

Longarm stood up then, Virginia following his lead. Coming around from behind his desk, Morgan peered with some apprehension at Longarm.

"Marshal, do you mean to say you think my janitor is a bank robber?"

"I'll know when I talk to him. But I suppose there's no way I can know for sure, unless he robs this bank."

Morgan appeared to shudder. "Mr. Long, do you know what that would mean to this bank, to this town?"

"I have a pretty good idea."

"Do you have any advice for me? Should I close the bank while you check on my janitor?"

"No. Keep it open. That would only warn those who are in this with Delsey. And it would unnecessarily alarm the townspeople."

Morgan nodded decisively. "You're right, of course."

"Just don't get panicky. I'll get back to you as soon as I talk to your janitor."

Morgan told Longarm he would do as he said, and seeming somewhat more relieved, he escorted them from the bank, bowing gallantly to Virginia as she passed out the door with Longarm.

"A shrewd old gent, that," Longarm said to Virginia as they started down the street.

"Yes, and *very* courteous. He's really an old dear, Custis. One of the few gentlemen in this town. He has always treated me with respect."

"You know that for a fact, do you?"

She laughed throatily and thrust her hand through his

arm. "Older men are so nice—I mean, so appreciative."

As they approached the Golden Slipper, Longarm said, "You don't need to go with me to the boarding-house. I'd prefer it if you'd just tell me how to get there."

"You mean you're expecting trouble?"

"It'll be easier for me if I don't have to worry about you."

They halted in front of the Golden Slipper. "All right, Custis," she said. "But please, do be careful."

"I didn't get this old being careless. There's still a chance this janitor might be only that, a janitor. Now how do I get to his boardinghouse?"

She told him how to get there. He thanked her, tipped his hat to her, and paused long enough to see her enter the Golden Slipper before continuing on down Main Street.

Following Virginia's directions, he cut down the next side street and after a few blocks caught sight of a neat brick rooming house across the street on a corner. He was about to cross it when Bud Gunther and Dutch Rawlings stepped out of an alley in front of him and planted themselves squarely in his path.

"Well now, lookee here," said Gunther. "If it ain't the U.S. deputy marshal."

Longarm halted. "What's on your mind, Gunther?"

"This here broken wrist. That's what's on my mind."

"I get it. You want me to break the other one."

Gunther's companion spoke up then. "We heard you got back without Decker." He was smiling, his bad teeth resembling a rotting fence. "And the Kid's been sliced up pretty bad. That's what I call real good news."

Without comment, Longarm started up again. The two men moved quickly forward to intercept him. Longarm stopped.

"You see how it is, Deputy?" Gunther said. "You ain't goin' nowhere. Not today, you ain't."

As he spoke, both he and Dutch drew their six-guns.

"Put away them guns," Longarm advised.

"Sorry, Deputy," said Dutch, still grinning. "You ain't gettin' past us."

"That's because we got some unfinished business to settle with you," Gunther advised.

Longarm was not at all intimidated by these two buffoons. What he felt instead was a monumental impatience. Furthermore, he was anxious to get across the street to the boardinghouse. A woman was walking alone on the other side of the street, her long skirt brushing the ground, a bright parasol resting on her shoulder. No one else was in sight, except for two elderly gentlemen in shirtsleeves and straw hats, who were sitting on a frame house's porch steps farther down. They were absorbed in a conversation, paying no attention to Gunther and Dutch as they drew down on Longarm. And any disturbance, Longarm knew, would simply cause the two men to bolt back into the house for cover.

He could count on no assistance from that quarter.

A surry turned the corner behind the two men and headed down the street toward them, its horse high-stepping smartly. On the bench seat sat two of Virginia's girls decked out in feathered hats and bright dresses. One of the girls, a feather boa draped around her neck, was driving the horse. Timing his move carefully, Longarm stepped closer to the curb and as the surry swept past, doffed his hat to the girls, bowing gallantly. The girls brightened at Longarm's gesture, while the one with the reins flicked them smartly, lifting the horse to a spirited trot, neither girl appearing to note the two men facing Longarm with drawn guns.

As the surry kept on down the street, Longarm turned swiftly back around and clapped his hat over Gunther's face, momentarily blinding him. He kicked Gunther high on his right knee, then turned and grabbed the barrel of Dutch's six-gun, twisting violently upward. As Gunther, clutching at his knee, collapsed to the sidewalk, Dutch tried to regain control of his gun. Longarm kept on twisting it upright. The big revolver detonated. Longarm smashed Dutch in the gullet with his clenched fist. Gagging violently, Dutch let go the revolver and clasped his neck with both hands. Staggering back, he dropped to one knee, trying desperately to suck air into his lungs. Longarm didn't think he had broken the man's windpipe, but he had sure as hell come close.

After reaching down and disarming Gunther, Longarm told both men to get up.

"We can't, you bastard," Gunther moaned.

Longarm kicked Gunther in the chops, flipping him over backwards. Gunther rolled onto his knees and peered blearily up at Longarm. "Jesus, what'd you have to go and do that for?"

"It's your big mouth, Gunther," Longarm told him. "You should watch what you call people, even someone as friendly as myself."

Gunther slumped back on his haunches without further protest. Dutch was still writhing on the ground, hanging on to his throat, an unpleasant gargling sound still coming from him. The two gentlemen in shirtsleeves farther down the street had come to their feet when Dutch's gun detonated and were now looking his way with some apprehension. Longarm waved them closer. They looked uncertainly at each other, then started to move cautiously toward him.

When they reached him, Longarm guessed the younger one was about fifty, his companion over sixty. To the younger he gave Gunther's six-gun, handing Dutch's gun to the older one.

"What's your name, mister?" Longarm asked the younger man.

"Abe. Abe Nichols."

"Abe, I want you to go get that new deputy sheriff."

Abe's eyes widened as he stared up at Longarm. "Hey, ain't you that U.S. deputy marshal?"

Longarm nodded. "That's right, and I want you to tell the sheriff that these two pieces of offal were disturbing the peace and when I collared them, they resisted arrest. Tell him I want them locked up."

Abe nodded obediently, stuck Gunther's weapon in his belt and hurried off down the street. Longarm turned then to his companion, who was surveying with pronounced distaste the two men sprawled on the ground before him.

"These two men are your prisoners," Longarm told him. "Cover them while Abe goes after the sheriff. Think you can handle that, old-timer?"

"Name's Cliff. Cliff Beacher. Don't worry, Marshal.

I handled worse than these two in my time."

"Good."

Longarm left them and crossed the street to Mrs. Fordham's boardinghouse. Glancing cursorily at the sign in her front yard, he mounted the neat brick steps and knocked on the front door. It was opened by a rose-cheeked, apple dumpling of a woman he assumed was Mrs. Fordham. A long apron protected her dress, and on the tip of her nose there was a tiny patch of flour. As she opened the door wide, the aroma of hot apple pie wafted out around her ample figure.

"Howdy, ma'am," Longarm said, touching his hat brim to her. "I'd like to see one of your roomers."

"Who would that be?"

"Del Johnson."

"Won't you come in?" she said.

"Yes, ma'am," Longarm said, stepping inside. "Thank you."

The landlady closed the door behind him and then led the way into her sitting room. Once there, Longarm turned to face the woman.

"Do I smell apple pie?"

She beamed. "Yes, you do."

"You're making it fresh for Mr. Johnson, I'll bet."

"It's his favorite."

"Well now, I think Del's a very lucky man, Mrs. Fordham."

She blushed.

"So why don't you go back into the kitchen and tend to that pie and let me go on up by myself and surprise Del. I haven't seen him in a coon's age."

"Oh, are you an old friend of his?"

"We go back a long ways. Is he upstairs now?"

"Oh, yes, poor dear. He came in late last night and told me he wasn't feeling too good, said he'd be staying in today, resting up. When I went up with some chicken soup earlier, there was a sign on his door. It said he was sleeping, and when I peeked in, sure enough, he was sound asleep."

"Which room is that, Mrs. Fordham?"

"It's on the second floor in back, next to the bathroom."

"I'll go up and bring him down. When he smells that apple pie, he just might hug you out of pure gratitude."

She uttered a delighted squeal. "Well now, you go right on up," she told Longarm, "and perhaps you would be kind enough to join us for dinner."

"That's very kind of you, ma'am."

As Mrs. Fordham left the sitting room and disappeared in the direction of the kitchen, Longarm returned to the hallway and, taking the stairs two at a time, ascended to the second floor. The sign Del Johnson had hung on the door was still there. Longarm knocked sharply. There was no response. Tossing away the sign he pushed open the door, and peering in saw Del Johnson still asleep in his bed, the covers pulled well up over his shoulder, obscuring his head. The only window in the room was closed, the curtains drawn.

Stepping inside the room, Longarm found the air in it close and fetid. Striding quickly to the side of the bed, he flung the blanket off the sleeping man. He stepped back, arms akimbo, not all that surprised, since no one could sleep through a day as hot as this one under such a load of bedclothes. It was not Del Johnson Mrs. Fordham had seen sound asleep in his bed, but a cleverly contrived dummy.

Her star boarder had flown the coop and was going to miss out on her oven-fresh apple pie.

Chapter 9

Two days later, as the doctor passed Longarm's table on his way out of the Golden Slipper, Longarm beckoned him over. The doctor changed direction and, pushing his derby hat back off his forehead, slumped wearily into a chair beside Longarm, welcoming with a nod the Maryland rye Longarm poured into a shot glass for him.

The doctor's name was Erasmus Dante, prompting everyone to call him Doc. He was a short, gray-haired man with a neatly trimmed beard and shrewd hazel eyes that peered out at Longarm through steel-rimmed spectacles. Most doctors Longarm had come upon during his years on the trail were a sullen, unkempt lot, for the most part lushes and in many cases opium addicts. This doctor was an exception. Remarkably abstemious for a bachelor, his frock coat and trousers were cleaned and pressed, his boots polished to a bright sheen. His person was immaculate, and he kept his hands scrubbed as pink as his cheeks—all this, according to Virginia, due to an odd notion the doctor had concerning something he called "germs."

"Been waiting for you, Doc," Longarm said. "How's the Kid?"

"Remarkable rate of recovery, if I do say so myself. The Kid must be made of Indian rubber." He smiled at Longarm, lifted the glass in salute, and threw down his drink. Smacking his lips, he said, "You, too, Deputy, I might add, seem to have recovered nicely. You were both lucky those knives severed nothing vital."

"I guess we were at that."

Longarm filled the doc's glass again. "How're them two reprobates I got locked up doing?"

"They'll live, more's the pity. I must admit, Long, this town has had a complete about face since word got around as to how you handled those two. Bullies, both of them. Been terrorizing this town for years."

"What about Dutch? Can he talk now?"

"He can, but it's quite painful for him to do so."

"And how's the other one?"

"Gunther? I took off that foolish splint he'd put on his wrist and bound the wrist tightly. He can use his fingers, so I don't think you did more than crack a few bones."

"So if I let them out, they'd be able to get around?"

"They would. But why would you want to do a thing like that?"

"Have to let them out sometime, Doc. I was hoping that attorney general from Lincoln would've got here by now; but as everyone in town knows, he was not on yesterday's stage."

"Do as you see fit, Deputy," the doctor said, finishing his drink, "but it certainly is more peaceful in this town with those two animals locked up."

"Maybe I won't have to, Doc, if you can tell me where Del Johnson might be hiding out."

"You sure he's still in town?"

"Yes, I am. He didn't take the stage yesterday and he's not yet ridden out of town. Chet's been patrolling the outskirts of town every night, hoping he might try to slip away."

"Afraid I can't help you. But if I hear or see any sign of Del, I shall be certain to contact you, of course."

"I'd appreciate it, Doc."

The doctor lifted his black bag off the chair next to him, stood up and left the saloon. Longarm carried his bottle of Maryland rye over to the barkeep and followed the doc out of the saloon. He watched the doc idly as he crossed the street, then descended the saloon steps to the sidewalk and set out for the sheriff's office. Striding into it a moment later, he found Chet dozing on his cot near the wall, his two prisoners staring sullenly through the bars at him.

Longarm shook the deputy sheriff awake. Chet sat up, scratching his head sleepily.

"What now, Longarm?"

"I say to hell with waiting for that attorney general or the circuit judge. Let these two reptiles out. Give us both a chance to relax."

"You mean let 'em out now?"

"No. Not right now. Give the town a break this afternoon, then let them out before supper. Save the county the price of two meals."

Gunther and Dutch had had no trouble hearing everything Longarm had just said.

"You goin' to let us out?" Gunther demanded.

"Looks like it," said Chet.

Gunther looked at Longarm. "Thanks, you son of a bitch."

Dutch, standing beside Gunther, made no effort to speak, content to glare venomously through the bars at Longarm. Longarm walked closer to the jail cell and looked in at the two men.

"You're welcome," he told Gunther.

Then he turned and strode from the jail.

As Longarm followed Gunther and Dutch, it soon became obvious they were heading for Lum Doubleday's Carriage Emporium at the end of the street. Cutting behind the building, the two men entered a yard filled with a confusion of buggies, traps, flat-beds, and farm wagons. Threading through the crowded lot, the two men disappeared at the back of it into an old, weathered barn.

Longarm had been tailing the two men since Chet released them a couple of hours earlier. First they had supped at a restaurant near the jail, then ducked into a nearby saloon, where their loud welcome turned finally into a minor brawl. After boiling out of the saloon, they had headed down this side street, and now, as the two men disappeared into the barn's gloom, Longarm was confident that he had finally discovered the two men's living quarters, something no one else in town would tell him. No one, it seemed, was anxious to get on these two rogue males' shit list.

Ducking into the barn after them, Longarm found himself picking his way through a confusion of overturned buggies and wagons, stepping onto torn and gutted leather seats, pushing past broken wheels and a foot-tangling thicket of axles and singletrees until he reached a rear stairway. Moving up it to a second-floor landing, he turned off it and proceeded silently down a narrow hallway, pausing at last in front of a closed door. A crack of a light gleamed under it, and from the other side came Gunther's loud, drunken banter, which nearly drowned out Dutch's painfully scratchy voice. Longarm heard as well the sound of beer mugs clashing against a moonshine crock as the two men continued their boozing.

So far, so good. Convinced that these two were in league with Del Johnson, Longarm had released them in hopes they would lead him to Johnson, who was holing up somewhere in town, and what better place than in Gunther and Dutch's digs? But now, listening patiently outside the door, Longarm did not hear any third voice joining in the raucous conversation.

For a decent interval Longarm listened at the door, hope ebbing as the two men's voices became more and more garbled. He heard Dutch curse, then one of them stumbled and went crashing to the floor, reducing a piece of furniture to kindling. Longarm was about to step back from the door and leave the two men to their own drunken devices when he heard, close behind him, the creak of a board.

Before he could turn, a small body slammed into him

with such force, the door in front of which he had been crouched splintered and swung open, hurtling him and his attacker into the room. Crunching to the floor on his back, Longarm found himself under a furious, driving little man. He had found Del Johnson finally.

"I got him! I got him!" Johnson cried. "He was outside, ready to break in."

As Longarm flung Johnson off him, he saw Gunther looming over him, a broken bottle in his left hand, a maniacal grin on his face. He swiped viciously at Longarm, the bottle's jagged edges sweeping past within inches of Longarm's face. At the same instant, a booted foot dug into the base of his skull. Lights exploded deep inside his head. He rolled away, his shoulder crunching through the legs of a table, which promptly collapsed down onto him. Shielded by the table's top, Longarm drew his .44. Dutch kicked the table top off him, and Longarm saw Dutch holding a jug over his head, ready to bring it down on his skull. Longarm fired up at him. The jug disintegrated, sending jagged pieces of crockery into his eyes. Screaming, Dutch grabbed his bloody sockets and spun about, plunging blindly away from Longarm. He slammed against the window. The window panes crumbled outward and the flimsy wall beneath the window gave way. Carrying a shower of window glass with him, Dutch vanished into the night. Still on his back, Longarm swung his arm around and was just in time to see Del Johnson vanishing out the doorway. Gunther, crouching by the door, rocked back, confused, staring at the hole in the wall through which Dutch had just vanished. He was still holding the broken bottle in his left hand. As Longarm aimed his .44 at him, he blinked furiously at Longarm, flung down the bottle, and vanished through the doorway.

Longarm scrambled to his feet. From the alley below came Dutch's low, terrified moan. Ignoring it, Longarm ran from the room, hoping to overtake Del Johnson. He had not gone far before he heard Gunther's sudden scream. It was cut off abruptly, then followed by a terrified, whimpering sob. Longarm kept going, and bursting from the narrow hallway saw where Gunther, in his haste to bolt down the stairway, had collapsed the railing, hurtling himself onto the forest of whiffletrees and axles planted on the barn floor. He had managed to impale himself on a whiffletree, its knob protruding from his back. Moaning softly now, Gunther writhed and twisted like a worm on a hook.

When Longarm reached Gunther's side, he saw a thick ribbon of blood flowing from a corner of his mouth. The man was cold sober now, his eyes tracking Longarm pleadingly.

"Shoot me," he gasped. "For God's sake, shoot me."

"If you were a horse, I would."

"Please!"

"I'll go get the doc."

"Bastard!"

Longarm pushed his way through the tangle of wagons. When he reached the barn's entrance, he caught a glimpse of Del Johnson running full tilt as he vanished into an alley across the street. Longarm glanced back at Gunther. In the barn's gloom he could barely make out Gunther's dim form hanging loosely, his head down. He was no longer screaming. It was already too late for the doc, Longarm realized.

Longarm circled the barn and found Dutch still twisting slowly on the ground. He had broken a leg in his fall, but all he seemed to care about was the fact that he had been blinded. Moaning in terrible fear, he kept crying out that he would never see again.

Longarm almost felt sorry for the man.

"What the hell's going on out here?"

Longarm spun about. A thick-set fellow toting a Greener had planted himself at the corner of the barn.

"Who're you?" Longarm demanded.

"That's my question, mister. This is my place. You're trespassing."

"Are you Doubleday?"

"That's me, all right."

"I'm Custis Long, a deputy U.S. marshal."

Doubleday peered more closely at Longarm, then slowly lowered the shotgun. "Yeah. I've seen you around town." He walked closer and peered down at the whimpering Dutch. "Who's this?"

"Dutch Rawlings."

"What happened to him?"

"He thinks he's blinded. Maybe he is. His buddy Gunther is inside the barn, a whiffletree growing out of his back."

"Jesus, Deputy, what're you up to?"

"Doubleday, didn't you know these two men were using your barn for a flophouse?"

He shrugged. "Sure. I knew. But I didn't have no appetite for tangling with them two apes."

"Then maybe you should get the doc to look after your two boarders. I got other business."

Doubleday nodded unhappily as he looked down at the sobbing Dutch Rawlings. Longarm hurried off. He still did not have Del Johnson, but he was sure as hell getting close.

Cyrus Morgan pulled open his door and looked up in some surprise at Longarm.

"Sorry to bother you at home like this, Morgan," Longarm told the banker. "Could I see you for a moment?"

"Why, of course, Deputy. Come right in."

Closing the door behind him, Morgan took Longarm's hat and dropped it on a hat tree in a corner, then led Longarm into his living room. A huge fireplace dominated the room. A quartet of massive buffalo heads were planted on the walls, and sitting in a wall rack over the mantle was a big Sharps buffalo gun. Longarm walked over to look at it more closely.

"Take it down for a look-see," the banker urged, his eyes twinkling.

Longarm did so and saw the words "Old Reliable" stamped on the barrel. He hefted the long rifle, enjoying its fine balance, his eyes caressing the gleaming octagonal barrel.

"What's it shoot?" he asked Morgan.

"Fifty caliber."

Longarm nodded. It was what he had surmised. "Use it much?"

"I'd like a nickel for every buffalo I cut down with it," he replied, gazing fondly at the weapon. "One stand I remember, I dropped fifty-nine buffalo with sixty-two cartridges." He shook his head ruefully. "Never thought

I'd see the end of those magnificent brutes. Hell, they covered the prairie like trees. But I guess now I shouldn't be surprised they're gone."

"No, you shouldn't. Not when you and so many others had weapons like this." As Longarm spoke, he placed the buffalo gun back up on the rack.

"Sit down, Deputy," Morgan said. "Make yourself comfortable."

Longarm folded his long frame into a seductively comfortable leather easy chair. Morgan picked his pipe up off the mantle and sat down in an easy chair across from Longarm.

"What can I do for you, Deputy?"

"I almost caught up with that missing janitor of yours, Morgan."

"Del Johnson?"

"That's what we'll call him, all right. But I'm pretty damn sure he's the John Delsey I came here to get."

"Only you didn't get him."

"Not yet."

"You want to tell me what happened?"

Longarm lit up a cheroot and told the banker about his visit to Lum Doubleday's carriage barn and its wild aftermath, with Del Johnson vanishing into the night. When he finished, Morgan got to his feet and began pacing.

"Where do you think he's gone?"

"I got some ideas. That's why I came here."

Morgan stopped his pacing and swung around to face Longarm. "Well?"

"Del Johnson's your janitor. That means he must have a key to the bank so he can get in early before you and the others. To start the furnace, maybe. To clean up. Am I right?"

"Yes, of course Del has a key."

"Does he have a room in the cellar, a place where he could rest up, maybe, with a cot in it?"

"Why, yes, he does. It's just beyond the boiler room."

"I'd like a key to the bank, if you have one you could lend me."

"Yes, I have one I could give you. But let me get this straight, Deputy. Are you saying Del might be hiding out in the bank right now?"

"He was moving pretty fast last I saw and he was sure as hell going somewhere."

Morgan frowned suddenly. "Deputy, this business with Del Johnson. I'm puzzled. What's this all about?"

"Don't you know?"

"I have my suspicions, but I want to know what you think."

"I think your bank is a target. Decker, Frank Carson and Gunther and Dutch were in on the heist."

"And Del Johnson?"

"He's the inside man. His specialty is opening safes."

"But the deputy's dead and Ben Decker's lit out. You don't think he'd try something now, do you?"

"I'm not sure. But I came here to get that man, and get him I will. So I'd like that extra key, if you don't mind."

"Of course. I'll get it for you."

Longarm was waiting at the front door when the banker brought him the key.

"This is for the back door," Morgan said, handing the key to him.

Thanking him, Longarm took the key and put on his hat. As he left the house, Morgan warned him to be careful, that Del Johnson might be dangerous. Longarm thanked him for his concern and hurried off, heading for the back alley that ran behind the Pawnee Wells National Bank.

Letting himself into the bank, Longarm closed the door silently behind him, then paused in the darkness to listen. He heard nothing. He struck a match and in its flaring light glimpsed an open stairway leading to the cellar. The match's light died and he flung it away and descended the stairs to the cellar.

Passing the boiler, he almost tripped over a coal shuttle. He kept on, feeling his way carefully in the darkness until he came to Del Johnson's room. The door was ajar. Pushing it all the way open, he slipped inside and lit another match. A lamp sat on a table by the cot. He lifted off the lamp's chimney and lit it.

Then he sat wearily down on the dusty cot.

The room did not look as if Del Johnson or anyone else had used it recently. He supposed it would have been too much to expect to have found Del Johnson asleep here in the room. But he did not let himself get discouraged. The night was not over. Leaning back on the cot, he turned off the lamp and closed his eyes. When, and if, Johnson got here, Longarm would be waiting.

He did not intend to sleep, but dozed off nevertheless. What awakened him was the sound of something thumping heavily down on the floor upstairs. Then came another sound, footsteps. Sitting on the cot, he cocked his head at the faint, unmistakable clink of tools.

Hell's fire! While Longarm was sleeping down here on Johnson's cot, Del Johnson was upstairs breaking into the bank's safe.

Longarm swung quickly off the cot and left the room.

Moving as swiftly as he could through the cellar's stygian darkness, he came to the stairs and mounted them to the bank's first floor. Crouching, he moved silently into the bank's lobby and saw a lamp sitting outside the door leading into the main vault. As silently as a cat, he pushed through the gate and moved behind the counter. Just inside the open door, he saw Del Johnson hard at work setting a charge in the safe door, a lamp sitting on the floor beside him.

No longer intent on concealing his presence, Longarm drew his .44 and moved closer to Johnson. But so intent was Johnson, he did not hear Longarm. Longarm was about to make his presence known, but before he could, Johnson lit two fuses and blew out the lamp beside him. Backing quickly out of the room, he nearly bumped into Longarm.

Johnson seemed irritated, not surprised, as he took up the lamp outside the door and waved Longarm back.

"I'm using nitro!" he cried. "Get back."

Longarm did not argue with the man and was huddled in a corner beside him when the charge blew. It felt as if someone had clapped his hands over Longarm's ears, and for a moment he had difficulty breathing. The safe door lifted off the safe, turned in mid-air and slammed sideways into the doorway, smashing it to kindling, while out of the vault room a thick, acrid cloud of smoke billowed, obscuring both men.

Johnson got to his feet.

"All right, Johnson," Longarm told him. "You've done enough. Leave what's in that safe."

Johnson turned to face him, an odd smile on his face. "Sure thing, Deputy. Glad to oblige. We was wondering when you'd show up."

"We?"

Smiling, Del Johnson nodded. "That's right. We been waiting for you."

Longarm heard movement behind him, but before he could turn completely, Del Johnson's accomplice brought the barrel of his six-gun down on the top of Longarm's head.

Longarm opened his eyes. It was morning. The sun was streaming in through the bank's windows and the head cashier was bent over him, peering down at him with obvious concern. As Longarm shook his head to clear away the ringing in his ears, the Kid entered the bank and bent quickly over him.

"You all right, Longarm?"

Longarm sat up. "Did you get them?"

"The bank robbers?"

"Who else?"

"Chet's forming up a posse."

"Didn't anyone hear the explosion last night?"

"Some did, some didn't. Those that did rolled over and went back to sleep." The Kid looked suddenly sheepish. "Like me."

Longarm pulled himself up onto his feet and looked over at the blown safe. It was as empty as a drunk's promise. Then he noted the ashen-faced bank employees and the crowd gathering in the street outside the bank. He saw pure despair on their faces and understood how they felt. The bank had been cleaned out, and those people standing there in the cold gray light of a new day had been wiped out.

"How much was in the safe?" Longarm asked the cashier.

"I can't give you an accurate sum, but I've sent for Mr. Morgan. He should know."

"It won't do you any good to send for Morgan."

"Why do you say that, sir?"

"Because it was Cyrus Morgan who robbed this bank."

Chapter 10

Later that same morning Longarm was sitting at his table in the Golden Slipper when through the front window he saw the posse with Chet at its head gallop back into town. From the hangdog look on the faces of the posse members, it was obvious they had raised a lot of dust and little else. Virginia and the Kid were at the table with him.

"Look at 'em," the Kid said. "Back already, and all they've done is chew up the trail."

Longarm agreed. His mood was sombre and a bit humbler than usual.

He blamed himself for letting Morgan get away with this. He should have suspected Morgan from the first.

The riders converged on the hitch racks in front of the Golden Slipper, and a moment later Chet pushed into the saloon slapping dust off his Levi's, the posse members following him in. As they crowded up to the bar, Chet came over to Longarm's table and slumped down. Virginia beckoned to one of her girls and told her to bring over another bottle of Maryland rye and fresh glasses.

"What did you find?" the Kid asked Chet.

"Nothing," Chet said glumly. "No sign. Just grass and sky."

"But they must be out there somewhere," said Virginia.

"Sure, but where?" Chet said to her almost plaintively. "Which way did they head out? North, south, west?"

"They were heading west when they left town," the Kid reminded him.

"Sure. When they left town. But after that, how can we tell which way they went? They're gone, I tell you, swallowed up by the prairie."

"Less'n they can fly," said the Kid, "they'll be leavin' tracks."

"On grass that thick?"

"If you know where to look, sure."

"That's Indian talk," Chet said resentfully.

The Kid smiled, sat back in his seat, and winked at Longarm. "Yes," he said. "It sure as hell is."

The doc pushed into the saloon. Virginia waved him over to the table. He arrived at about the same time as the fresh bottle and glasses. He greeted everyone cordially in turn, then eased himself into a chair, placing his black bag on the floor beside him.

"How's Dutch Rawlings?" Longarm asked him.

"He'll have some sight in his left eye, I reckon.

146

Enough to get by on. But he'll have to wear a patch over his blind eye like his late lamented friend. I gave him Gunther's eye patch to try on, as a matter of fact."

"How's he takin' it?" Virginia asked.

"Like you'd expect, whining, blubbering."

"I wouldn't wish no such luck on any man," said Chet, "but it won't hurt me none to think of Dutch quieted down some. He gave me holy hell them few days he spent in the lockup."

"Who's goin' to bury Gunther?"

"No takers yet, and Dutch is claiming poverty."

"I'll do it," said Virginia, filling the doc's glass.

Everyone at the table looked at her. She saw their astonishment, and shrugged.

"Hell, he spent enough money in here to pay for half my new mahogany bar," she told them. "I guess I owe the poor dirty son of a bitch that much. And it'll be a relief to see him gone for good and all. May God forgive me."

"He will," said the Kid. "Don't you worry none about that."

The doc finished his drink and wiped his mouth with the back of his hand. "How much did Cyrus take with him," he asked Longarm. "I been too busy to hear the details."

"At least fifteen, maybe twenty thousand."

"Jesus, Mary, and Joseph," the doc said reverently. "That much?"

"That much. Some in bank notes, but most of it in silver. Eagles and double-eagles."

"That's quite a load to be carrying in a hurry, isn't it?"

"You're damn right it is," said the Kid.

Longarm glanced at him, an eyebrow cocked. "Looks like you're talking from experience."

The Kid grinned, but said nothing.

"But why did he have to blow up his own safe?" the doc asked. "Surely he knew the combination of his own vault."

"He got himself one of them newfangled time locks a couple of years ago, and couldn't unlock the vault until this morning, a little while after the bank opened for business," Longarm replied. "Things've been falling apart since I got here, so he's had to bide his time. When I came to his house to get a key to the bank, he must've figured it was time for him and Johnson to make their move, when they could take me out at the same time."

"And you walked right into it," said the doctor.

Longarm nodded in glum agreement. "I walked right into it."

Chet shook his head. "All that money, gone. Taken by Cyrus Morgan! I can hardly believe it."

"I can," said Virginia gloomily. "He was always a shrewd old cuss. There was a lot more to him than met the eye."

"When are you going out again, Chet?" Longarm asked.

"You kidding? The posse's disbanded. I never saw such a sore-ass bunch of faint hearts. Hell, if you ask me, I think they were glad we didn't come up on that old fox. They know all about that buffalo gun of his."

Longarm glanced at the Kid, a question in his eyes. The Kid nodded. Longarm looked back at Chet.

148

"Stay in town," he told him, "and keep a lid on things. That attorney general from Lincoln should be in soon. Maybe he'll keep you on."

"Where you goin'?"

"After Morgan and Johnson."

The Kid got to his feet. "And we're leavin' now."

The doc looked at the Kid. "You sure you're up to it?"

"If I stay in town much longer, I'll be a dead man."

"How come?"

Virginia laughed and rested a hand lightly on the doc's wrist. "It's Annie. Since we put the Kid in her room, she's taken a real interest in him. Maybe it would be better for both of them if the Kid moved out for a while."

"Oh." The doc chuckled. "I see."

The sun was a white hole in the sky. Huddled by a water hole, Longarm and the Kid were sucking in great gutfuls of air, leaning back on their elbows. They had emptied their canteens over their heads first thing, then filled the crowns of their hats with water and put them back on. Due north of Pawnee Wells, the Kid had picked up Morgan's trail. This had not been easy for the Kid. The posse's tracks had almost entirely obliterated Morgan's tracks. Now, after stretching their horses to the limit, they had halted to take stock.

"Only two horses," the Kid reminded Longarm, "and they're ridin' flat out."

"Those aren't cow ponies they're riding," Longarm reminded the Kid. "They're English saddle horses."

"Don't make no difference," the Kid insisted. "They

149

couldn't be going that fast carrying all that silver. They must have stashed it somewhere."

Longarm nodded. It was the only explanation that made any sense. The two bank robbers had been lengthening their lead throughout the morning, while their own mounts were close to collapse.

Longarm screwed shut the cap on his canteen, walked over to his horse and tied it to the saddle horn. At the same time he took a long look at his mount, a powerful chestnut, the best the livery had to offer. As it stood there in the sun's blazing heat, it was still breathing hard and flecks of dried foam still clung to its chest.

Abruptly, Longarm looked back at the Kid. "The thing is, Kid, we've been forgetting what Cyrus Morgan used to do for a living."

"He hunted buffalo. Selling hides is where he made his fortune."

Longarm went back to the Kid and hunkered down beside him. "I've heard where them skinners dug out a hole in the prairie near a watering hole, covered it with a framework of saplings and prairie sod and then spent an afternoon picking off the buffalo that came to drink."

The Kid sat up and thumbed his hat back onto his head. "Sure. I know all about it. That's how them bastards slaughtered all our meat, killed off the great herds."

"Well, this old buffalo hunter we're after has dug himself another hole in the ground."

The Kid came alert at once. "Hey, I been noticing something, but I wasn't sure it meant anything."

"What?"

"Them two started off due west, but they've been

150

drifting to the south for the last couple of hours. If they keep on the way they been going, they'll have doubled back."

"To Pawnee Wells?"

The Kid nodded.

"They're coming back for the silver then, to the spot where they cached it."

"Let's go meet them," the Kid said, getting up and reaching for the reins to his horse. "My guess is they'll be heading for a spot close by Pawnee Wells, near where we cut their sign to begin with."

Close to midnight, north of Pawnee Wells, Longarm and the Kid pulled to a halt. Two riders and a flat bed were off to their right, both riders and wagon standing out with sharp clarity in the full moon's light.

"Looks like they're loadin' up that wagon."

"Morgan must've cached it somewhere close by."

The Kid chuckled. "Let's go get 'em."

They hadn't ridden more than halfway before one of the riders left the wagon to ride swiftly toward them. Within a couple of hundred yards he dismounted, flung himself down in the deep grass and began sending a steady volley at them with his Winchester. From his slight build, Longarm guessed the rifleman to be Delsey attempting to give Morgan time to load up the wagon. Delsey didn't possess the same skills as a marksman that he did as a safecracker, his rounds going either too high or plunging into the sod yards in front of the two men.

Longarm and the Kid separated, dividing Delsey's fire, then coming at him from two directions. Aiming at

Delsey's gun flashes, Longarm and the Kid poured a steady volley at him. Soon the rapid fire from the prone figure came to a halt; and when Longarm and the Kid reached the man, he was little more than a bleeding piece of earth.

Dismounting then, they left their horses behind and started for the wagon. They had not gone far when Morgan's big buffalo gun barked, the muzzle flash coming from a spot just to the rear of the wagon.

Longarm could almost hear the slug coming.

He and the Kid both dove sideways. A Sharps in the hands of an old buffalo hunter was nothing to take lightly.

"Hang back," Longarm told the Kid. "Let me go first. The two of us together make too good a target."

The Kid nodded curtly, darted off to Longarm's left and was soon out of sight in the tall grass. Longarm started cautiously forward then, waiting for Morgan's next blast. His Sharps outranged Longarm's Winchester by at least half a mile, which meant Longarm needed to get to within a couple of hundred yards before he could open up on Morgan. The one advantage Longarm had was that the Sharps was a slower, single-shot breech-loader, and though it threw a monstrous ball one hell of a ways flat, at this distance it took a while for the tracer to reach its target. It was this fact that Longarm counted on to enable him to dodge each round, then jog forward a good distance while the man reloaded.

The muzzle flashed.

This time Longarm darted to his left, then raced forward as the round plowed the ground a few feet away to his right. When the next muzzle flash came he broke this time to his right, the tracer plunging to the ground even closer. It was obvious Morgan was attempting now to anticipate which way Longarm would jump. It was not a pleasant task this, and Longarm was grateful for the distraction offered by the Kid laying back in the grass. He was keeping up a steady nuisance fire, causing Morgan to send a few occasional rounds in his direction. At least five more times Morgan sent a fifty caliber round at the oncoming Longarm, the Sharps's awesome tracers arching closer each time.

Not less than a hundred and fifty yards from the wagon, Longarm flung himself flat on a sandy knoll, which gave him a clear shot at the wagon and the figure behind it. Slipping off his safety, he tucked the Winchester's stock into the hollow of his right shoulder and waited for the Sharps's next blast, hoping that maybe this one would be directed at the more distant Kid. When it came, however, Longarm was the target, the round's flat trajectory burning toward him with astonishing speed. He could hear it searing the night air as he rolled swiftly aside and felt the round plow into the sand only inches away, sending up a shower of rock and sand that pelted his back.

Quickly propping himself back up on his elbows, he again fitted the Winchester's stock to his shoulder. Just before the muzzle flash he had glimpsed a shadowy figure at the front of the wagon, and aiming at that spot, squeezed off a shot; levering rapidly, he put another round close in after the first, and then another. And still another. He thought he heard a distant cry, but could not be sure and kept on pouring fire at the spot.

Then he held up and waited.

After a short, nervous wait, Longarm saw the Kid rise up from the grass off to his left and trot cautiously toward the wagon. Longarm rested his sights on the wagon, hoping for a moving target, but there was none. Nor was there any return fire as the Kid kept on coming. Seeing this, Longarm got to his feet also and trotted across the moonlit prairie to the wagon, reaching it just a few strides ahead of the Kid.

Behind the traces the dead banker was sprawled on the ground, half his head blown away, his hand reaching out one last time for his buffalo gun. Dropping to one knee alongside him, the Kid gave Morgan a quick, cursory examination, then stood up and walked over to Longarm.

"Looks like you got him in the side first before you blew his head off. I'd call that pretty fair shooting."

The Kid was right; it was good shooting, all right, but it gave Longarm little satisfaction. He wished the banker had made it possible for Longarm to take him alive.

Longarm turned away from the dead banker and looked into the wagon. Morgan had already dumped ten bulging saddlebags and a strongbox into it. From the look of them, it was obvious the saddlebags contained the silver, while the strongbox was probably filled with the bank notes Morgan had taken. Two large carpetbags and three trunks had also been dumped into the bed of the wagon.

Moving away from it, Longarm and the Kid explored

the surrounding prairie, and less than ten yards from it came upon a deep trench dug out of the bottom of a swale. It was into this that Morgan had evidently driven the wagon, after which he had roofed over the trench with rough two-by-fours, which he had covered in turn with squares of prairie sod.

The Kid shook his head in rueful admiration. "That old fox sure worked hard on this."

Noting how smooth and dry the sides of the trench were, Longarm said, "I'd say he dug this trench months ago. He was in no hurry. He could've taken a buggy ride out here any dark night and dug a few feet each time."

"It sure must have taken a few trips," the Kid said.

Longarm glanced back in the direction of Pawnee Wells. "And he's far enough away from the trail cut by them trail herds so there wasn't much chance a stray steer would crash through the planks covering the wagon."

"Or any curious cowpoke," the Kid added.

The two men turned away from the trench and headed back to the wagon. It was ready to pull out; all that was needed was for the two English saddle horses to be backed into the traces and harnessed.

A half hour later Longarm and the Kid drove the wagon into Pawnee Wells, pulling up alongside the undertaker's. The Kid hopped down and set out to rouse the undertaker while Longarm walked across the street to get Chet to go find Frank Wells, the bank's chief cashier.

There were bank notes and many shining piles of

silver to be counted, then returned to the coffers of the Pawnee Wells National Bank, so that when morning came the citizens of Pawnee Wells could breathe easy again.

Christmas had come early this year.

Chapter 11

Halfway through the next morning, Virginia fluffed and rearranged her pillow, then propped herself up onto it, doing absolutely nothing to conceal from Longarm's gaze her breasts' generous opulence. She knew full well the effect this display was having on him, which was, of course, why she provided it. Watching her, Longarm wondered how he could possibly rise once more to the temptation she was offering.

"But Custis, I don't understand," she said, shaking out her hair.

Her dark coils of hair cascaded down past her alabaster shoulders, a few curls coiling teasingly about her erect nipples.

Longarm forced himself to look away. "Understand what?"

"How was that old dear going to get away with it? What was his plan?"

"The way I see it, Morgan planned to stash the money in the wagon, then let Delsey and Decker blow open the safe. When the gang members saw that the vault contained only an empty strongbox and precious little silver, they would have known they had been tricked. They'd have no choice but to light out. With them gone, Morgan would have given a very different account of how much had been in the safe when it was blown. Later, when the dust cleared—a month, maybe two months later—Morgan would simply ride out one dark, moonless night, hitch up his wagon full of silver and bank notes, and be on his way, with no one the wiser."

"You mean he knew all along who Del Johnson was?"

"I'm willing to bet he was the one who brought Delsey to Pawnee Wells in the first place, then conned Decker and the others into taking part in the robbery. He probably told them he would join them later to pick up his share after they made good their escape."

Virginia's eyes gleamed with sudden comprehension. "But Decker and the others would have no intention of sharing their take with Morgan. They would take the money and keep on going."

"That's precisely what Morgan counted on to sell Decker and the others on his plan. And they went for it. They figured if Morgan was that dumb, he was ripe for the plucking. They didn't suspect a thing. It's hard to be wary of a man you think is a fool."

"Custis, if you hadn't shown up when you did, I do believe Morgan might have succeeded."

"Maybe."

"I'm almost sorry he didn't."

"I know you liked the old fox, Virginia," he said. "So did I. But don't forget, he had thrown in with Ben Decker, who was responsible for the cold-blooded murder of Pete Krueger."

Properly chastened, she reached out for him. "I'm sorry, Custis. I just didn't think. Will you ever be able to forgive me?"

He laughed and, scooting up beside her, flicked his tongue over one of her nipples. Laughing seductively, she embraced him. A moment later, to his pleasant surprise, Longarm found that he was not as completely spent as he had thought.

It was late in the afternoon and Longarm was on his way out of the Golden Slipper when the boy from the telegraph office burst through the batwings looking for him.

Longarm took the telegram, tipped the kid, and ripped open the envelope. The telegram was short and very much to the point:

FORGET DECKER STOP RETURN TO DENVER STOP
WHY DO YOU KILL EVERYONE I SEND YOU AFTER
STOP FORGET DECKER STOP VAIL

Longarm crumpled the telegram and flung it into a spittoon. It was the answer he had expected, but not the one he had wanted. He had telegraphed Vail, asking for permission to finish his assignment by bringing in Ben

Decker. Pushing out through the batwings, he paused on the saloon's porch. Annie was sitting in a rocker at one end of it, a stein of beer cradled in her lap, tears streaming down her cheeks.

He walked over and sat down beside her. "What's the matter, Annie?"

"Nothing, Mr. Long."

"Do you usually sit out here and drink beer by your lonesome and cry for nothing?"

She wiped her nose with the back of her hand. "It's the Kid."

"What about him?"

"He's gone."

"Gone? Gone where?"

"I don't know. He said he was going after somebody."

"Did he say who?"

"Said he was going after the bastard who killed old Pete."

"Hell, Annie, he's still cut up too bad to ride that far."

"Don't you think I know it? I spent near an hour wrapping bandages around him. But he wouldn't listen to me."

Longarm turned back into the saloon and hurried up the stairs to get his gear and say good-bye to Virginia. On his way out of town he would instruct the telegrapher to wire Vail that his telegram had not been delivered, that Longarm had already left town.

He wasn't going to leave Ben Decker to the Kid alone.

. . .

The rifle in the rocks spoke again. From where he sat his horse on the ridge, the Kid heard a loud whack as the round slammed into the side of the wagon rattling along the floor of the basin. On the wagon's seat, the old man—a prospector from the look of the tools hanging along the wagon's side, and the two forlorn mules pulling him along—glanced up to the slope toward the rocks where the rifleman lay hidden, then turned back around and kept going.

The Kid's horse flung its head around, the crack of the rifle nearby making it a mite nervous. Maybe the horse was right, the Kid reflected, maybe he should just keep going. He had other fish to fry.

The rifle below in the rocks cracked again. The grizzled old-timer lifted the reins to whip the mules on, but in his haste he wasn't steering very wisely and the wagon's left front wheel slammed into a large boulder embedded in the ground. There was a crack, the spokes snapped, and the wheel's rim went rolling off into the brush as the wagon bed slammed down, plowing a few feet along the ground before the mules halted.

Peering down, the Kid saw a tendril of smoke curling up from the rocks, pinpointing the rifleman's position. The Kid swore as he watched the sniper, who was positioned behind a boulder jutting out of the mountainside, tuck his rifle stock snugly into his shoulder and sight on the wagon again.

The bastard had already done enough damage. What the hell was he up to now? But even as the Kid asked himself the question, he had his answer. This was all just pure, mean-spirited deviltry. This son of a bitch with the rifle was having himself a good old time shooting up the old prospector's wagon.

And maybe even the prospector himself, if it came to that.

The Kid studied the mountainside, noting several ravines and a stand of piñon that clung to a gravel slope. If he chose to, he could slip down there and get pretty close without revealing his presence to the sniper. He thought about it for a minute. This business wasn't any skin off his nose. It was Ben Decker he had come to these badlands to find.

This fact sobered him. His blue eyes took on an expression of flinty withdrawal, and looking away from the unpleasant business below him, he urged his horse on up the slope. The rifle below spoke again, its sharp crack echoing on the surrounding rocks. The Kid kept on, trying to ignore it. But the idiot below him would not let him as he fired again. And then again.

With a resigned sigh, the Kid slipped off his mount and tethered it in a clump of bullberry. He drew his rifle out of its sling, levered a cartridge into firing position, and picked his way down toward the rocks. Despite the acres of bandages that Annie had wound about his torso, he moved with an easy, effortless grace, like a large cat. It took him ten minutes, keeping always in cover, to reach the rocks just behind the rifleman. Kneeling behind a granite upthrust, he drew a bead on him. The man's attention was riveted on the old prospector, who was crouching fearfully down on the other side of the wagon by this time.

"You like to shoot up old men, do you?" the Kid

asked, speaking just loud enough for the rifleman to hear him.

The fellow didn't move. Without turning his head, he said, "Who wants to know?"

"Put down that rifle."

"Why should I?"

"I've got a rifle trained on you—and that old man's a kin of mine."

"Shit! That crazy old fart down there don't have no kin."

"He does now."

The man hesitated, then set the rifle on a rock slab behind him and turned his head to look up at the Kid. He was a solidly built individual with bloodless lips and pale-green, dead-looking eyes in a pocked face. The collarless calico shirt under his black leather vest was a dirty gray at the neckline. The only clean thing about him was the Bull Durham tag dangling from his vest pocket.

He wore his gun tied down in an oiled, flapless holster.

"Keep your hands up where I can see them," the Kid said, picking his way over the uneven slope down to him.

"How'd you get in so close?" the man asked, a faint contempt glimmering in his eyes. "What are you, some kind of breed Injun?"

"You're goddamn right I am. Stand up."

The man did as he was told, slowly, warily. "This here ain't none of your business. What do you care what I do to that old fart? He's a goddamn cheat."

"Turn around."

"Leave me be and I'll forget this. Let it end here and you won't get in any deeper. You can turn around right now and ride out of here and I won't hold no grudge."

"That's real white of you. I said turn around."

The man turned.

"Take off your belt."

The man let his gun belt sag to the ground.

"Where's your horse?"

"Over in them rocks."

"Go get it and ride out of here."

"What about my hardware?" the man said. "That's a Colt and .44-40 Winchester layin' on the ground."

"Leave 'em."

The man turned to regard the Kid. Then, forcing a smile, he turned back around and walked off, heading for the spot where he'd left his horse. The Kid watched him disappaer into the rocks and a moment later saw the man astride a pale gelding pick his way down the slope to the floor of the basin, then ride off. The Kid turned then and walked over to the rifle and flung it into some rocks farther down the slope, after which he kicked the gun belt into some bushes.

Angling down the slope to the prospector, he found him still crouched on the ground behind his wagon, staring with dazed misery at the wheel-less axle. At the Kid's approach, he looked mournfully at him, then got slowly to his feet. He seemed composed entirely of bone and gristle. His large, mournful eyes were sunken into deep sockets, his lips folded in around almost toothless gums. On his bald head sat a black, floppy brimmed hat.

"Who're you, mister?" he asked.

"Never mind that. You all right?"

"Yeah. I guess so. Looks like I'll have to ride back in to Black Cliff on one of my mules to get me a new wheel."

"Which way's Black Cliff?"

The prospector gestured back down the basin. "About four miles."

"Can you make it back all right?"

"I done coped with worse than this in my time, sonny."

"You know who that was up there shootin' at you?"

"Ruel Hartung, if I'm any judge."

"How come?"

"It ain't none of your business, sonny, but since you bought your ticket you might as well know what's on the playbill. I won big from him in a poker game, and he thinks I cheated."

"Did you?"

The old man grinned, revealing great gaps in his teeth. "Maybe I shoulda said he *knows* I cheated."

The Kid turned and started up the slope to his horse.

"Sonny. . .?"

The Kid looked back at the prospector.

"Thanks. If you hadn't butted in, Ruel might've finished me off just to get these mules and some of his money back. I owe you."

"Forget it, old man."

"Name's Summers. Jim Summers."

"So long, Jim."

Scrambling back up the slope, the Kid untied his horse, mounted up and headed off. He was still on the trail leading to Black Cliff a half hour later when he heard the click of a horse's hoof against stone coming from behind a patch of timber beside the trail. He looked over and saw a big, round-shouldered man with a flat, pushed-in face ride out from the timber. Three more riders followed out after him and all four closed quickly around the Kid, grins on their hard-bitten faces. Then a fifth rider joined them, the pockmarked rifleman the Kid had just sent packing, minus his rifle and six-gun.

The prospector had said his name was Ruel Hartung.

"It's him, all right," Hartung told the big, round-shouldered rider. "I knowed it was him soon's I saw he was a breed."

"You're right, Ruel." The big man shook his head in wonder. "This here's the Pawnee Kid, all right."

"Who're you?" the Kid demanded.

"Me? Why I'm Charlie Decker, and these other three are my brothers. Ben's waitin' at the ranch house. He'll be real glad to see you, Kid, cause the damn fool thinks he already killed you."

"He tried, and that's a fact."

"Well, now," Charlie Decker said, chuckling. "Nice of you to let Ben and the rest of us finish what he started."

Charlie Decker's brothers crowded about the Kid, quickly disarming him; then they lashed his hands to the saddle horn with rawhide. Grabbing the reins to the Kid's horse, Ruel Hartung pulled it along behind him as Charlie Decker and his brothers rode deeper into the badlands with their captive.

• • •

It was a day later when Longarm sighted the old prospector's wagon below the trail, moving in an odd, jerky fashion over the basin below him. He would not have paid it any heed if it had not been for its odd, irregular motion, and pulling up, he slapped the dust off his thighs and peered down at it.

The driver's two mules were doing their best to cope with pulling a wagon in which only three of its wheels were of the same size. The fourth wheel was at least a foot shorter in diameter, with rope and torn pieces of cloth wrapped around the rim in an effort to increase the wheel's circumference. This makeshift device was not very successful, however, and as the mules pulled it along, the wagon dipped and rocked crazily.

Watching the wagon move past below him, Longarm reached for his canteen. Tipping it up he was rewarded with barely a trickle. The other canteen was empty as well. Glancing about him, he saw no sign of trees or heard any sound that indicated a stream. Looking back then at the wagon, he had a sudden thought. Turning his horse, he let the animal pick its way slantwise down the slope.

Once Longarm reached the trail, he lifted his horse to a lope and overtook the wagon. Coming alongside, he asked the old man to hold up. Reluctantly, the prospector leaned back on the reins, halting the wagon. Mopping his brow with his bandanna, Longarm dismounted, noting as he did the fresh bullet holes in the wagon's side and canvas cover.

"I'm dry, mister," Longarm told the man. "Got any

water in them barrels strapped to the side of your wagon here?"

"I guess maybe I have," the old man allowed, getting cautiously down from his seat.

His bones were brittle, obviously, and so thin was he that it seemed to Longarm that he was activated by invisible strings, like a puppet. His mournful eyes were sunken into deep hollows.

Longarm had the old man fill his hat first so he could slake the horse's thirst, then, using the old-timer's wooden ladle, he filled his two canteens, careful that he not spill a drop of the precious liquid.

Longarm thanked him as he handed back the ladle, then slung the canteens over his saddle horn.

"What's your name, old-timer?"

"Jim. Jim Summers."

"What happened to your wheel?"

"Broke it. Went back to Black Cliff, but couldn't get another one the same size."

Longarm swung up on his horse. "I'm a stranger in these parts," he said.

"I knowed that."

"I'm looking for the Decker clan, Ben Decker in particular."

The old man squinted up at him. "You a lawman?"

Longarm reached into his coat, pulled forth his wallet, and showed the man his badge.

"If I'da known you was a U.S. deputy marshal," he sniffed, "I wouldn't a given you no water."

Longarm laughed. "Glad I didn't let on then. So I guess that means you won't help me?"

"I already done that. I gave you some water."

"Just tell me where I can find the Deckers' place."

"Don't see why I should. I got enough trouble already, what with one of Decker's pals fixin' to ventilate me."

"Why would he want to do a thing like that?"

"Caught me cheatin'."

"At cards?"

"Yep."

"He the one shot up your wagon?"

"Yep."

"Then why wouldn't you want me to bring him and Decker in?"

"Because you can't do that. You'd only get me in worse trouble. That's why I'm pullin' out. That clan's the law hereabouts, and that badge won't help you one bit, 'cept maybe give them fellers a nice, bright target to shoot at."

"I think you're exaggerating, Jim."

"Maybe so, but they already took care of one poor breed bastard what stuck his nose in."

Longarm came alert instantly. "What's that you say?"

"You heard me. The poor son of a bitch disarmed the man what was taking pot shots at me, and now the Deckers've got him, accordin' to what I just heard in Black Cliff."

"You say it was a breed who helped you?"

"He was a breed, all right," the old man insisted, sending a black dart of tobacco juice at the ground. "He had Pawnee blood in him if I'm any judge."

"And you say the Deckers've got him?"

"Yep, the poor, meddlin' fool."

The old-timer climbed back up onto his wagon seat.

"Hold it right there, Jim," Longarm told him. "I think maybe you're going to have to tell me where I can find the Deckers' ranch."

The sharp edge in Longarm's voice was enough to convince the man to cooperate, even if he was a lawman. The Deckers had a ranch a few miles due west of their present position in what was called Devil Butte Canyon.

"How long a ride is it?" Longarm asked.

The prospector looked shrewdly at Longarm's mount. "I reckon you might get there by nightfall."

Longarm thanked him and rode off in the direction he had been given. Looking back just once, he managaed to catch a glimpse of the prospector's wagon disappearing like a crippled cockroach into the badlands' wild, serrated landscape.

He kept on through the fierce heat of the day, grateful for the sweating canteens from which he allowed himself an occasional sip. Late that afternoon, as he approached Devil Butte Canyon, he found that the prospector's directions had been right on target. Following a meandering stream, he entered the canyon, its high cliff walls shutting out the sun, plunging him into a cool, premature evening.

Once past the canyon entrance, he dismounted and led his horse on foot, keeping close in to the canyon wall. As he crossed an open stretch still hammered by the late-afternoon sun, his boots just missed lizards scuttling for cover, abandoning the parched ridges of brown grass dotting the hard-packed ground. A jackrabbit fled from him in great, soaring bounds.

Rounding a shoulder of rock, he looked across the

flat and caught sight of three buildings—a house, a bunkhouse, and a barn. He made out corrals behind the barn and saw a few horses grazing farther down the canyon. The stream he had followed into the canyon crossed just in front of the ranch. Anyone approaching from that quarter in daylight, across a treeless open space bordering the shallow stream, would immediately alert anyone in the ranch house.

Pulling his horse back in behind a cluster of rocks, he slumped down with his back against a boulder, tilted his hat down over his face and closed his eyes. He would rest up some and wait for darkness before crossing that open space.

The moon was turning the night sky pale just beyond the mountains when Longarm ducked around the corner of the bunkhouse and peered at the ranch house. He was close enough to reach it with a thrown rock. The bunkhouse he had already checked out and found empty. The light coming from the ranch house's two front windows stamped the littered front yard with bright rectangular patches.

The door swung open. Light spilled across the porch and down the steps into the yard. A man Longarm did not recognize appeared on the porch and emptied a full slops jar, not bothering to heave it any great distance. The sound of the wet contents slapping the ground, together with its stench, came clearly to Longarm. The fellow turned to go back into the house and Longarm caught a quick glimpse of his sallow, pocked face.

Waiting only a minute or so longer, Longarm ran to the side of the house, flattening himself against the wall. From inside came the lazy hum of voices. Moving along the wall, he came to one of the side windows and peered in cautiously. The pock-faced man who had just dumped the slops jar was standing behind a table, watching the four men playing poker. Facing Longarm was a big, round-shouldered fellow with a face that looked as if it had been struck by a frying pan. All the other men at the table resembled Ben Decker vaguely; but where was Decker? Then Longarm moved to the other side of the window and, peering past the table, glimpsed Decker lying on a couch, his leg from the thigh down swathed in bandages, a crude crutch leaning against the wall beside him.

He had found the Decker clan, then. But where was the Kid?

Longarm moved past the widow, and turning the corner found two rear bedroom windows. Peering into each one, he could see little beyond mussed beds and an opened closet door. He kept on until he came to a corner window and peered into it, finding a room not much larger than a closet. He thought he saw a cot with some-one sleeping on it. He could not be sure, however, so thick was the grime covering the windowpane. He wiped off as much of the dirt as he could with his hand-kerchief and found himself looking into a small tack room, a wide selection of harnesses, reins and bridles hanging from pegs along one wall. As his eyes grew accustomed to the tack room's dark and clutter, he was able to make out more clearly the figure of the man sprawled on the cot. As soon as he did, he swore.

He had found the Kid.

His stomach wrenching at what he saw, Longarm pressed his face close against the windowpane. The Kid's wrists were tied to hooks on the wall behind him, his ankles to the foot of the cot. His shirt was gone and his chest was covered with bloody, lengthwise stripes that reached clear across his chest, the mutilation extending clear down to his waist. To amuse themselves, it seemed, the Deckers were systematically peeling strips of the Kid's flesh off his chest, slowly skinning him alive.

Pulling back away from the window, Longarm forced himself to calm down. When he did so, he again pressed his face to the window to see if the Kid was still alive. But he was in shadow, so Longarm, concentrating his gaze on the Kid's ravaged chest, could not make out for sure if he was breathing. After a few minutes he was able to see it rising and falling steadily. The Kid was still alive—but not by much.

Longarm pulled back from the window, his thoughts racing. He had to act and act fast; but he was dealing with at least six men. Though one of them had to rely on a crutch, he could still shoot a six-gun.

Longarm needed the Kid's help.

He tried to lift the window sash. It was stuck fast. Years of encrusted dirt held it securely. His desperation gave him enough strength to nudge it upwards a few inches, but that was all. Stepping back, he grabbed his rifle and shoved the barrel in under the sash and pried it up a few more inches. Putting aside his rifle, he grabbed the bottom of the sash and heaved upward. The window went up slowly, steadily, until it was high enough for him to thrust his shoulder in under it and climb into the tack room, pulling his rifle in after him.

The Kid's eyes were closed, but when Longarm leaned over him, his eyelids flickered, then opened. The Kid had enough presence of mind not to say anything. Instead, incredibly, he smiled. Longarm took out his pocketknife and cut through the rawhide thongs binding his wrists and ankles.

Gritting his teeth, the Kid sat up.

"What kept you?" he whispered hoarsely.

"Jesus, Kid. You look terrible."

"I don't feel so good and that's a fact."

"You want to help me get these bastards?"

The Kid grinned at Longarm. "You're goddamn right I do."

Longarm gave the Kid his Colt. "I'm going back outside. I'll come back in through the front door without knocking. Can you get in there to back my play?"

"I can make it."

"Don't show yourself until I kick in the door."

The Kid nodded and, gritting his teeth, pushed himself upright. For a moment Longarm thought he was going to pitch forward onto the floor, but he reached out and grabbed the doorjamb. Longarm waited while he steadied himself.

"You sure you can cover me?"

"Just get back out that window," the Kid said.

Longarm squirmed back out through the window and dropped to the ground. He looked back into the tack room. The Kid's shadowy figure was moving out of it. Levering a fresh cartridge into the Winchester's firing chamber, Longarm ran swiftly around to the front of the house and charged up the porch steps, his booted right foot smashing against the door panel with such force the panel splintered, the door slamming open. Charging on into the ranch house, Longarm burst into the living room, his rifle leveled at the amazed card players.

"Don't go for your guns!" Longarm warned them.

But they had no intention of letting him get away with this.

Knocking over the table, they flung themselves to the floor and went for their guns. The big, round-shouldered fellow had his Navy Colt drawn even before he hit the floor. He fired up at Longarm, the detonation filling the room, his slug crashing into the wall behind him. Longarm fired down at the man, opening a neat hole in his shirtfront, just as a fusillade came at Longarm from all sides. Dropping to one knee, he levered swiftly and returned the fire, catching one of the Deckers in his gun hand and blowing the hat off another one. At that moment the Kid lurched into the room and clubbed one of the Deckers to the floor.

The Kid's appearance quieted the others dramatically. Losing all enthusiasm for further battle, one of the men dropped his gun and got slowly to his feet, his hands over his head. Ben Decker had not left the couch. The one who'd taken a slug in his gun hand remained on the floor, clutching at it as he rocked back and forth. The big fellow with the Navy Colt remained on his back, dead as a doornail, his eyes staring sightlessly at the ceiling. The one the Kid had clubbed from behind struggled slowly to his feet, and the pock-faced gent Longarm had watched empty the slops jar remained standing in the corner, his weapon still in his hand, the gun barrel pointing down at the floor.

"Drop the gun, Ruel," the Kid told him.

Ruel did as the Kid instructed.

Longarm looked over the room. Counting Ben Decker there were still four reasonably healthy men watching him and the Kid very carefully, waiting for the chance to rush them.

Longarm glanced over at Ben Decker. "You're coming back with me, Decker, for the murder of Pete Krueger."

"You must be crazy. I got friends. You'll never get out of the badlands alive. Besides, I can't ride."

"You'll ride. Or you'll walk."

Longarm took back his own .44 from the Kid and handed him a Colt he found on the floor. "Cover them while I collect their weapons."

Working quickly, Longarm gathered up the Deckers' side arms and piled them on the table, then searched the rooms for more weapons, turning up three rifles and a carbine. In two quick trips he took them outside and dumped them into the privy. Gathering up what rope and rawhide he could find in the barn, he returned to the house, and with the Kid still covering them, bound Ruel Hartung and the Deckers. That accomplished, he and the Kid dragged the men into separate rooms, gagged them, and locked the doors.

Afterward, the Kid found a jar of axle grease in the barn and smeared it over his mutilated chest, easing somewhat the steady flow of blood that oozed from the long, ugly wounds. Then slowly, painfully, he eased his shirt down over his chest. This seemed to help some, but to Longarm the Kid appeared dangerously weak, and he was worried he might not be able to make it all the way back to Pawnee Wells.

As the Kid disappeared inside the barn to saddle their horses, Longarm went back into the house to get Ben Decker. Decker's hands had been bound behind him, and this Longarm had assumed would be sufficient, since he was in such poor condition. But when Longarm returned to the living room, he found the man off the couch, hobbling painfully toward Ruel Hartung's bound and gagged figure. In a few moments he might have been able to help Ruel free himself.

The moment Longarm appeared, Decker stopped his awkward struggle to reach Hartung and let himself slip sideways onto the floor.

Longarm peered coldly down at him. "Get up."

"I told you, I can't."

"Fine. We'll bind your legs together and sling you over the horse like a sack of grain. It's a long ride, so whatever you got in your stomach you'll probably lose."

This unpleasant reality took the starch out of Decker. Reaching back, he used his crutch to pull himself upright, and with an alacrity that did not surprise Longarm in the least, lurched out of the ranch house ahead of him.

Outside, the Kid was standing by the two horses he had selected and saddled. Leaning on his crutch, Decker halted a few feet in front of the Kid.

Longarm was puzzled.

"Where's the third horse, Kid?" he asked. "I need a horse, too. Mine's on the other side of this canyon."

"We don't need a horse for this bastard."

Reaching back, the Kid unholstered his Colt and

fired twice into Ben Decker's chest. Letting go of his crutch, Decker slipped to one side, then slamming heavily to the ground, an amazed look on his face, his eyes opened wide in death.

"Kid!" Longarm cried. "You had no right to do that!"

"I'm an outlaw," the Kid reminded Longarm. "A rustler and a horse thief. That gives me all the right in the world."

"No, it don't, Kid. Nothing gives you the right to shoot down a man in cold blood. And Ben Decker was in my custody."

"Decker was skinning me alive. Him and his brothers. He told me he was getting even for every white man killed by a Pawnee. He was hoping my skin would last a week, maybe longer."

"Goddamnit, Kid! I know you got a reason for what you done. But now I'll have to take you in!"

"No, you won't."

His Colt pressing urgently against Longarm's solar plexus, the Kid slipped Longarm's .44 from his crossdraw rig and stuck it in his belt, then clubbed Longarm solidly on the side of the head. Longarm's knees turned to water as he sprawled forward to the ground. But he was not completely out, and as he felt the Kid move past him, he managed to palm the derringer from his vest pocket.

The Kid was climbing the porch steps. In his parlous condition, it was not an easy task for him.

"Hold it right there, Kid," Longarm rasped.

Reaching the porch, the Kid did not pause.

"I got a bead on you, Kid!"

The Kid spun to face Longarm and raised his gun.

Longarm hesitated, then fired. Twice. But his senses were fuzzy from the blow to his head and he was not sure if either round had found its mark. Turning back around, the Kid vanished into the ranch house. Longarm tried to get up and go after him, but the sudden exertion caused his head to spin even more violently than before.

Two quick shots sounded from within the ranch house; after a pause there came a third and a fourth. Longarm heard the crash of a kerosene lamp from inside as the Kid flung it against a wall; a moment later tendrils of black smoke began coiling out through the open door. Flames began flickering in the windows.

The Kid, carrying Longarm's .44 in his hand, emerged from the ranch house. Longarm managed to push himself to a sitting position. The Kid, moving with some difficulty, descended the porch steps and halted beside Longarm's sprawled figure.

"Goddamn," the Kid said, peering down at the lawman. "I forgot all about that damn belly gun of yours."

"You kill every one?"

"Yep."

"So now it's my turn."

"That's right."

Rocking slightly on his heels, the Kid aimed carefully down at Longarm. But he did not pull the trigger.

"Go ahead, Kid," Longarm told him. "If you don't finish me off now, I'll be coming after you."

"Aw, hell, Longarm," the Kid said, dropping the .44 to his side, "you know I ain't goin' to shoot you."

"If you don't, you're a dead man."

"I'm a dead man already."

As he spoke, the Kid slumped to the ground by

Longarm, his head sagging forward. It was then Longarm saw the gaping hole his round had opened in the Kid's chest. The Kid offered no resistance as Longarm took back his .44.

The billowing waves of heat thrown off the ranch house were growing more intense with each passing second. Longarm slung the Kid over his shoulder and carried him a safe distance away from it, putting him down gently at the base of a small cottonwood. The saddled horses standing by the house were becoming more skittish with each passing moment, and Longarm hurried over to them and led them back into the barn.

When he returned to the Kid, he found him very still. He shook him gently first, then more vigorously, but he could not rouse him.

The Kid was dead.

As the flames from the Decker clan's funeral pyre turned night into garish day, Longarm slumped to the ground beside the Pawnee Kid.

Chapter 12

Longarm brought the two beer steins over to the booth and sat down across from Vail. Thanking him, Vail pulled his beer closer, took a sip, then wiped the suds off his chin with the back of his hand.

"So here's the payoff," he said. "We made a deal with the Nebraska attorney general. He's mad you didn't wait around for him, and he thinks you have a tendency to leave too many bodies behind, but he won't press charges, no matter how loud that Texan cattleman screams for your ass. But you were linked with the Kid, don't forget, and he was making a career of bleeding those trail herds. So you'll have to stay out of Nebraska for a while."

"Jesus, Billy. I don't know if I can handle that. What about that sheriff I installed?"

"Looks like he's the new sheriff. From what I hear, he took to the job like a duck to water."

"I should get some credit for that. I'm the one who stole his horse and made him sheriff."

"That ain't all, Longarm. Before I came over here, I got a wire from Washington. As far as they're concerned, the Decker clan massacre was the Pawnee Kid's doing. So that leaves you in the clear."

Longarm sipped his beer. "Anything else?"

"Yeah. I'm giving you a vacation. Starting tonight."

"Why?"

"I think you need it. You came back all cut up, talking to yourself. And I think I know why."

"Do you now?"

"The Pawnee Kid. You didn't like being the one who stopped him."

"Do you blame me?"

"Aw, hell. He was a notorious horse thief and rustler. His sidekick Tommy Black Eagle was wanted for murder in North Dakota."

"The Kid saved my life and I saved his. And I liked him."

"So all right. I can understand that. But it's dangerous to like some people. You ought to know that. So I'm telling you to put it behind you. What's done is done."

"No more lectures, Billy. Get me an assignment and I'll be fine."

"I want you to think of this vacation as your next assignment."

"Damn it, Billy. I don't feel like a vacation."

"Just hear me out."

182

Longarm picked up his beer and peered closely at Vail. "Okay. Let's have it, Billy. What're you up to?"

"Turn around."

Longarm did so. Virginia Colbert was standing in the Windsor Hotel's lobby entrance. The wasp-waisted, bottle-green dress she had poured herself into was cut so low only the ample swell of her breasts held it up. So startled was Longarm at the sight of her he almost spilled his drink as he put it down and waved to her. She waved back and started for the booth.

"She came to see me this afternoon," Vail told Longarm, slipping out of the booth. "Wanted to know if I could give her some idea where she could find you. I told her I thought I might be able to do that."

With a wave he left Longarm. On his way past Virginia, he tipped his hat; she responded with a dazzling smile. Longarm got up and took her hand, his lips brushing the back of it gallantly as he sat her down opposite him.

"This is a most pleasant surprise, Virginia."

"Thank you, Custis. My, it's good to see you again. How are you?"

"Fine."

"Really?"

"Of course."

"I'm glad to hear it. That nice Billy Vail said you've been feeling a mite poorly since you got back."

He smiled warmly at her. "Well, not anymore. You've just taken care of that."

She blushed with pleasure. Longarm could not help noticing that a great many of the men—those at the bar and some in the booths—were finding it difficult to keep their eyes off her.

"You're a long way from home, Virginia."

"You know, Custis, you didn't come back to Pawnee Wells to say good-bye."

"Sorry about that."

"So I decided what I needed was a shopping trip to Denver. Omaha was getting to be such a bore."

"Where are you staying?"

"Here, at the Windsor."

"Do you have your room key with you?"

"Yes. In my purse."

Longarm stepped out of the booth. "I promise you, Virginia," he told her, "this shopping trip will not be a bore."

She slid out of the booth also. "But we don't have to go shopping right now, do we?"

For the first time that day, Longarm laughed, and then assured Virginia that there would be plenty of time for them to go shopping. Later. Right now it was first things first. Taking Virginia's arm, he swept out of the lounge with her and headed for the hotel lobby's wide stairs, eager to start on Billy Vail's assignment as soon as possible.

Watch for

LONGARM AND THE DEVIL'S STAGECOACH

135th novel in the bold LONGARM series
from Jove

coming in March!

LONGARM

Explore the exciting Old West with
one of the men who made it wild!